Alpha Landon

Midika Crane

Inkitt

Chapter One

I push through the long grass, ignoring the sting and itch it gives my legs. I feel my thighs burn with the exertion. I can see his figure, not far off. He stumbles closer, but his ankle gets caught in a long piece of grass, and he trips over his face first.

Seeing him brings a smile to my face every time. It's not just the friendship we share, but the deeper feeling that has been growing for five years now. Of course, he sees me as just a friend, and I'm pretty positive he always will. But I continue to hang to every moment we get together, while neither of us are mated.

I burst out laughing, as I flop down beside him. He sits up, rubbing his forehead. He looks up at me through thick rimmed glasses, giving me a lopsided smile. His smile seems to light up more than the massive globe that slowly lights up the sky. The grass sways around us in the slight breeze, brushing against my covered arms.

"Graceful," I comment, letting my chuckles die down. He straightened his thin, lanky legs in front of him. He's wearing shorts, which is odd for this time of the morning. His fashion sense has never been the best, but the quality is impeccable.

Landon always complains about how he isn't very strong, or attractive as the other males he went to school with. He's a little too skinny, his eyes are sometimes too lifeless, and his hair never stays in one place for very long. Popular or not, I see Landon as an extremely generous, sweet guy who's ego isn't related to the size of his biceps.

This is where my best friend Landon and I always meet up; in the grass paddock that is situated right at the end of pack territory. Today though, he didn't seem to burst with whatever had happened in the palace he lives in. Usually the news is exciting and brings us more than a few laughs.

The thought of living in a palace, surrounded by many opportunities like Landon has seems like a dream. But it's his reality, and sometimes I wish his stories were something I could experience one day. Too bad I wasn't born into the power of an Alpha family like he was.

1

"So, excited for tonight?" I ask curiously. Tonight is his nineteenth birthday party, and the day he will turn into my new Alpha. He sighs and looks off across the paddock. I know him well enough to know he is distracted. And Landon distracted is never normal.

For years he's been anticipating this day. I don't blame him... Imagine being able to do what you want, rule a pack and become seemingly stronger. I realize this will taint our friendship, especially since his need to find a mate to help him rule he pack becomes more of a priority.

"Not particularly," he mutters, sweeping a hand through his soft brown hair so it flops over his forehead. I've always loved his hair, especially the way is shines under the warm sun. Only I notice the way those few strands of golden hair entwine around the rest. I wouldn't call myself obsessed, just more of an observer.

"Why not? This is what you have been dreaming about since you started school," I say truthfully. He has always told me he was bullied at his school for being twig thin and useless. Everyone had told him he would never become Alpha because he's too weak.

That stuff hits him hard, and now I can tell he's becoming more anxious, and is over thinking. He's doesn't need to, though.

"I'm not Alpha material," he sighed, picking at the grass by his side. I tilted my head, then shook it. He can't be serious. I watch him form a pile in front of him. He knows his way around the pack, and has been capable of ruling one since he turned 13. Even his father believes, and his father scares everyone in this pack.

"You know you will phase? Think of everyone who won't," I state. I myself am forever stuck in my awkward body. And I know for sure that once he shifts, I'll be just a sad memory of his childhood. I can imagine the girls all over him, wanting a piece of their Alpha, while I sit on the side, unnoticeable.

"Yeah..." he drawls.

"And when you become Alpha, I can see you more, right?" I ask, punching his shoulder. Landon's father is strict, and doesn't like that he'd has a girl for a friend. Just like my father dislikes Landon's company for me. Some days I wish less people would be so negative toward us.

It's not socially acceptable for males and females to be friends. Especially at our age, where finding a mate should be our main focus.

"Of course, it's just... well father said I'll be super busy and all. And as soon as I'm phased, I'm supposed to find a mate," he muttered, sighing deeply. I felt a sting in my heart. It still hurts hearing him talk about mates. I know that he doesn't mean to intentionally, he's completely oblivious.

The thought of him with a mate just makes my heart sink.

"Well, then you're just going to have to find a mate who doesn't mind us being friends," I state, flashing him a smile. He nodded. We both know how unlikely that is, even if now we refuse to voice it.

"You're going to forget about me... when you find your mate," Landon said gently, pulling his glasses off. I can barely imagine a life without my little Landon. I watch him rub the lens against his shirt. I can't believe that for a second he would think that I would ever ditch him, I mean he's more bound to ditch me for some beautiful girl.

"I never will, you're my best friend," I insist. He smiles and ruffles my hair. I love it when he does that... I silently revel in it for a moment.

"Good. And you're mine," he stated. I let out a deep breath. *You're mine.*

"So, you're going to be my Alpha," I say, giggling. His deep brown eyes lit up at my words. That's it, I knew he's excited for becoming Alpha, and there is no way he can hide it. He slips his glasses back on. It's a big deal, considering the Power pack is sometimes considered the leading pack. We've stopped wars, or, we've won them.

"Now you will have to obey me," he teased. I pretended to groan in disappointment. That doesn't sound too bad, actually.

We sat in silence for a bit, watching the sun rise. This is my favourite part of the day, and not just because I get to see Landon, but because everything is so open and free, and nobody is here to judge us. Deeper into the pack, things are less fresh and colourful. Army camps are a common sight within the Power pack.

"And your Dad, does he have a mate planned for you yet?" Landon asked randomly. I lay back, hiding my face behind my hands. Of courses does, that's all he seems to care about at the moment. A lovely, proper mate that is simple, *normal.*

"His name is as Jake. Total douche, goes through girls like he has them at an endless supply," I mutter. He's my Dad's friend's son. Apparently, Dad trusts him, so there goes my choice.

"Oh well. I guess I'm better go get ready for tonight," Landon said quickly, standing up. He brushed himself off. I suddenly didn't want him to leave me here. I know he needs to get ready, but I cling to every moment with him, and a few more wouldn't hurt.

I'm not sure if he's upset by my words, but he never really leaves so abruptly.

3

I watched him go, ambling and picking his way through the thick grass. I sighed, running a hand through my thick hair, wishing time would stop, so Landon wouldn't change, and we wouldn't have to find mates.

I trudged slowly back to my house. It's common for street fights around here, because some people just don't know how to keep their fists to themselves, so when I didn't see any, I was quite shocked.

"Why's it so quiet out?" I ask, dumping my coat on the chair. My father sat around the dining table, shovelling down the breakfast mother had cooked him. They were both in fluffy robes, with their feet clad in slippers. Breakfast is a family affair, that is quite a chore. Dealing with their generic conversations gets more than old.

"Everyone's preparing for the Alpha's son's birthday," father stated, picking up a newspaper. I combed my hair out of my face, and sat down. Dad knows exactly who it is that is taking the Alphas position. His hate toward Landon is something I struggle to comprehend.

"He's not just the Alpha's son, he's Landon and my best friend," I snap. Father rolls his eyes, taking a sip of his extra black coffee. It's early in the morning, but he gets today off work. Apparently, it's a public holiday on Landon's birthday.

I still remember how we met.

Dad was curious about why the palace was having such a big celebration. Landon was turning seven, and the festival was open to the public. Dad dragged me along, and I met Landon. We were best friends ever since he stole my ham sandwich.

"I'm sure he won't mind you meeting your new mate at his birthday then," he said blandly, watching as I took piece of toast from mother. I only ate toast at breakfast, especially if it's coated in butter.

"I'm not mating Jake," I respond, biting into my toast lathered with melted butter.

"No not Jake, Cyrus. He wants to go to the Wisdom pack, so he's smart," father proclaims, obvious proud of his findings. Great, another nerd whose attention span revolves around the laws of physics. Just great...

"No, thanks."

"Give him a try, you'll love him," dad states, giving me a lopsided smile. Maybe if I meet this loser, dad might cut me some slack. And I mean it's Landon's birthday, his, not mine. Dad is adamant about me finding a mate this year, and sometimes it's easier to let him have his say, and go with it.

"Yeah okay. Look, Missy wants me over at hers to get ready," I inform them, immediately dismissing myself from this boring conversation. I grab my coat, and head out. Ever since I graduated, the parents have been less strict about where I'm going at what times. Thank God...

It's still early, but I'm sick of father's attitude toward this whole mating thing. I get that he wants me to mate someone successful, but I should have a choice. I *am* the one who has to spend the rest of my life in his presence after all.

It's not a long walk before I make it to Missy's. I had dumped my dress there earlier, so no matter what, father had to let me go. Missy is a good friend. She helped me out back in High School, and even though she doesn't know me like Landon does, she's still super cool and easy to talk with.

Her house is a little quaint cottage, with a well-trimmed garden. My families garden is over run with weeds and vines, because my mother prefers to cook over garden. I walk up the path and to their door, before knocking.

Missy answers, a large smile on her face that had me slightly apprehensive. She hauls me in, slamming the door behind me. I'm dragged to her room in record speed, barely even uttering a small hello to her mother, who was baking in the kitchen.

She's an incredibly excitable person, and hopes to one day move to the Freedom pack and find a mate. She doesn't think she belongs here, and I don't blame her.

"I am so excited," Missy squealed, closing her bedroom door behind me. I've always been envious of her room, so spacious a modern. She flops down on her bed, grabbing a glossy magazine from under her pillow, before flipping it open hastily.

I warily perch next to her. Biting a glossy lip, Missy holds the magazine to my face, pointing to a picture with some girl.

"I am going to do your hair like this," she decided. I clutch my thin black hair, wondering if it will even make it into that fancy updo.

"Uh, I'm not sure that's going to work..."

"Oh, come on Althea, let me try," she pleaded.

I groaned, as she ripped a comb through my hair, obliterating ever knot with each tug.

By the time she was done, my scalp was raw, my eyes watering ever so slightly. I watched her try do a couple of small braids, before trying a new approach.

"I'm meeting my soon to be mate tonight," I say casually, watching Missy's eyes widen. Her eyes always glistened with excitement as soon as I even mentioned mates. She knows my father's motives, and my endearing

5

crush on Landon. She's still adamant that we will end up together, but I assure her it's unlikely.

"I knew you two would be together. Your children will be so perfect!" She gushed, her fingers still entangled in my hair. My eyes widen. Sex with Landon? Never really thought much about that. It made me squirm nervously.

"Not Landon. His name is Cyrus," I correct her dryly. Her face falls.

"Oh...but you and Landon though. He's going to get so much hotter tonight," she stated. I rolled my eyes. She knows what I'm like, how I prefer I personality over looks.

The party was supposed to start after midnight, so Landon could shift in the privacy of his home with the support of his family. He tried to convince me to come along, but his father thinks very little of me. And after midnight parties are practically normal for us Werewolves.

"Which means he's going to have every unmated She Wolf hanging off him tonight. He *will* forget my existence eventually, and in that time, I will have to find a mate." I sigh, picking at the end of my fingernail. Getting over a crush I've had on Landon for years won't be easy on my heart, so I'm trying to mentally prepare myself.

"Lucky for you, your best friend is a matchmaking genius who will *not* let you leave that party till you admit your love to the oblivious boy," Missy decides, jamming a hair pin into my hair viciously. I wince in response, holding in the profuse amount of swear words I would love to let loose.

Time will tell, fate is fate. I'm not Purity pack member, but I've managed to convince myself that he will choose who he thinks suits him best.

I just hope it's me...

Chapter Two

I pull my hand from Missy's sweaty grasp, rubbing it down the side of my dress. Her moral support is nice, but she is adamant about finding Landon. Sometimes I think she sees more faith in Landon and I's relationship than I do, personally.

"I'm supposed to be looking for Cyrus," I argue, as Missy drags me through a tight crowd of dancing people. We have just arrived, and it's just past midnight. Landon is nowhere to be seen, and neither is my supposed date. I'm hardly nervous about meeting Cyrus. I'm slightly tempted to shoo him in the direction of another girl, and I know Missy would feel obliged to help out.

"Stuff Cyrus, we have an Alpha to look for," she dismissed. I stop, yanking her back. I wanted to check on Landon, I mean he's my best friend. But, he's probably dealing with other important things at the moment. And anyway, this will be a tense time for his family, and I don't want to get in the way, or upset them.

"I need to meet this Cyrus okay? I'll find Landon later. Now go and have fun," I insist, trying to gently push her away by the shoulders. She sighed, and I could tell she was torn. She's cool to be around, and being alone in crowds is daunting, but I'm afraid she's going to get in the way.

"Fine, but we leave together," she states firmly. I nod in agreement, yet not quite feeling it. She's sure to find some male to take her home since she's currently unmated, and there is an abundance of handsome Wolves at her disposal. And with those legs, and that dress, she's quite the catch.

She skips off, and I decide to make a beeline for the refreshments. Apparently, Cyrus is trying to find me according to father, and maybe this will be a focal point for him. I wander around the table for a moment, refraining from getting a glass of punch from the massive crystal bowl.

The party is in full swing, with dancers and music filling the room to capacity. Many are intoxicated, and flopping around the floor with little to no coordination.

I gaze around, tugging at the ends of my thick, tight dress. The ballroom I'm situated in is decorated and bedazzled, the past Alpha showing off their substantial amount of wealth. Only he, a former party man would go to the lengths of this current affair.

"God Al, I've been searching for you for ages..."

I look up in time, just before smacking into someone's broad chest. I blink, looking up blankly. A handsome man stands over me, dark, smoldering eyes burning into mine. I swallow nervously. I've never seen him before, although he looks oddly familiar. That floppy brown hair... but that perfectly sculpted body is unfamiliar.

"You have?"

He called me Al, and only very few people know that. Wait... it can't be.

"Of course I have," he says, looking confused. I watch his dark eyebrows knit together, and I tilt my head. What is this guy even playing at?

"Yeah... Cyrus, right?"

"Cyrus?"

"Yeah, this is our date remember..." I inform him, wanting to snap my fingers in front of his face. He blinks in confusion, then a brooding, angry look forms on his eyes. I didn't mean to be so straight forward; did I offend him?

"Althea, it's me. Landon," he says slowly. It takes a moment, before hitting my chest like a jab. I stumble back a bit, my eyes raking up and down his body. Woah, woah... this can't be...

"Seriously?" He looks a little hurt, like I should know who my best friend is. But the thing is, I knew he would change, but not as substantially as this. Wow, he's not even wearing his glasses anymore.

"I... I mean, where are your glasses?"

"They broke when I shifted, but it's not like I really need them anymore," he responds. He's obviously proud about his change, but I'm finding it harder to accept. What happened to the boy I played games with all my life, who I grew up teasing, yet loving. Even his voice is deeper!

"I can't believe it's really you," I marvel softly. He smiles briefly, before grabbing my arm between his large, soft hands. I go to protest, as he begins to lead me away from the swarm of people, but I'm curious to see what he wants.

"We need to talk in private," he explains. I notice that his father is nowhere to be seen at this point. He leads me up a flight of stairs, and I take note of his lavish attire. His suit must have been recently custom made, considering her never used to be of such strong build.

The upstairs is dressed in a fine array of fabrics and furnishings, that my family could never afford. I'm lead into an office of sort, which room temperature is seemingly colder than down stairs, with all the sweaty, dancing bodies.

Landon seems discomforted, as he turns around, his eyes meeting mine.

"Althea..." he breathes, and my heart stops momentarily.

"How did this happen?" I gesture to his person. He frowns slightly, so creases forming on his forehead. He's the definition of an Alpha now, like he would fit in with the rest of them, even if he *is* the youngest.

"I phased. You were right, I'm better now," he concedes, a smile lighting up with face. I'm struck by his indifference. There is a bitter, sour taste in my mouth. Is he the same Landon, because if not, he's surely not better than before.

"Better? Landon-"

I was cut off, as the door to the office opened with a loud creak, making Landon and I jump visibly.

Fierce, intimidating and plain angry; Landon's father stood at the door. I'd met him one before, and at that time, he had yelled at me for intruding into his son's life. Ever since his presence has scared me, so making a break for the door seemed like a pleasant alternative to the situation.

His face is edged with scars, or as Landon explained; are what he calls lines of knowledge. He's been this packs Alpha for years, and apparently saw the War.

Years ago, Werewolves lived together, as one massive unity. That was until one Wolf decided he wanted to split from the pack, and be his own Alpha.

Many fought to the death, till eventually thirteen packs were formed, believing in different things. They followed their own rules, but every month, the Alpha's meet in the middle, and discuss the happenings of the packs.

"Landon! What are you doing alone with an unmated She Wolf?" Landon's father, Clarke's voice abruptly entered my thoughts. My vision shot up, to where Clarke's brooding glare shocked me into submission.

"Father, she's my friend," Landon argued. Landon's size was considerable compared to his father's. The Alpha blood that runs through him allows him to no longer cower to his father's stern words, but to come back with a response equally stubborn.

"How many times have I told you! Stay away from my son," Clarke yelled, turning the frightening conversation back at me. I blinked, surprised by his outburst. Sure, I should have listened, but I *do* love Landon, even if our father's hate the 'barely there' relationship we share.

"I'm sorry sir," I respond meekly. No use standing up for myself. It's smarter to be reasonable, especially around two hot headed males. One ex Alpha, and one Alpha. I could feel the heat in the room, see Landon's clenched jaws and fists, see Clarke's rapid breathing.

"Where's Georgia?"

The conversation was directed back onto Landon. Georgia must be another girl Landon's been paired with. Was she beautiful? Blonde, perhaps brunette? Tall, or maybe even short?

"Downstairs, with her girlfriends," Landon muttered. It couldn't be more obvious that Landon was frustrated that we had been interrupted from a crucial conversation that could further make or break our friendship. It was true, though. Because I wanted to sneak out the door before Clarke sent his son to his room, or something slightly more drastic.

"I should go..." I excuse myself. Landon frowns and shakes his head at me, while Clarke curtly nods. I reach for the door handle, but Landon's hand on my shoulder stops me. I shiver; it feels so good when he touches me.

"Al, don't go," he says softly, but his voice is stern. I shake him off. No way am I sticking around to hear the inevitable argument that's about to go down.

I slip out the door, ignoring the protests I could hear Landon throwing me through the door. I sighed, running my hand down my face. The party will run through till later morning, but who knows how long Cyrus will be here for.

Reluctantly, I gather my wits and trek downstairs.

I can see Missy across the room downstairs, dancing with some blonde-haired man. She looks like she's having great fun, while I'm stuck in a glum mood.

I wander around for a while, praying time would go faster so o could kick off these heels, when I felt a soft hand on my shoulder.

"Look Landon, I don-"

I trail off, turning around to see it wasn't really Landon behind me. Dark blue eyes gaze at me from behind clear glasses. He smiles at me warmly.

"Althea, right?"

I swallow, my mouth suddenly going dry. I nod slowly, not able to take my eyes off his. His forehead is covered with soft looking black hair. He tilts his head slightly.

"Nice to meet you, I'm Cyrus," he introduces himself. I'm a little surprised. I expected Cyrus to be a total geek coming from a guy that wanted to be in the Wisdom Pack.

I continue to blink, unable to form proper sentences or even words. I'm never this shy around many people, but for some reason, Cyrus is intimidating.

"So, you're the girl father won't stop going on about," he mused, chuckling softly. Of course. I bet my father and his father have been setting us up for a while now.

"I guess so," I mutter. He smiles in response showing off his dazzling white teeth. He suddenly takes my hand, making me jump. I can't help but compare his touch to Landon's.

"Shall we dance?"

I nodded slowly, pushing Landon out of my head as I allowed him to lead me onto the dance floor.

Chapter Three

I sit, the long grass surrounding me. I run my fingers through it, my eyes gazing out across the extensive space, looking for him. I've never felt so lonely in my life, as I sit here, wondering what I had done. An anger inside of me is brewing, and a kind of disappointment. I thought he was supposed to be my best friend...

This is the fifth morning since Landon's birthday, and not once have I seen him. We are supposed to meet here every morning, but I guess he has bigger priorities. He promised, which was the worst thing for my feelings. He said that we are supposed to meet here as long as we were friends.

I don't know what has empowered me to continue coming here, to wait for him. Obviously, I'm beyond livid, and I guess I just want to give him one last piece of my mind. If only he would show up so I could do exactly that...

Suddenly a figure appears across the meadow. I watch Landon, step over the fence wires with ease. Only around a week ago, he struggled to pull his legs over. A part of me is happy he's changed. For his sake, I mean. Sure, any girl cannot help being attracted to him, I mean, he's an Alpha.

I blandly watch him stride over, a look of angst on his face. He really has changed. He's so much bigger now, more intimidating. With every step he takes in my direction, my mouth begins to dry, and I wonder how I'm going to approach this subject. His long legs eat up the distance between us quickly.

Conversation usually flows with ease between us, but now it's like a handsome stranger is approaching me, and I'm a nervous wreck. I look away from him, staring out across the expanse of the field. I hear his footsteps trample the soft grass.

Without a word, he takes a seat beside me.

"It's been awhile," I start. My feelings are under control, but my voice is still a little shaky. It's the symptoms of keeping anger inside me, ready to burst out when least expected. Landon sighs audibly, then gently takes my hand.

I jump a little, startled by his gesture. I glance at him, to see him smiling at me softly. I shake my head and tear my eyes away.

"Would you like to know why I've been away?" He asks. I'm wary, and I know he's going to jump to some story that he believes will fix our friendship. He's done it before... I've always forgave him because I've been afraid he would leave me, and our friendship would be no more.

I shrug in response.

"I'm sorry I never told you, but I guessed you would understand... I went to the Alpha Meeting!"

Silence.

His mouth is split into a big grin, showing off his dazzling set of teeth. He's proud, and I don't blame him. Being able to meet all the Alpha is something *anyone* would want. But yes, he should have told me.

"That's great Landon," I mutter, forcing my lips to quirk up in a resemblance of a smile. He let go of my hand, and the absence is slightly depressing.

"Alpha Dallas is as intimating as they say, and Alpha Kaden is scary as hell," he rambles. Both are leaders of well-known packs. I nod along, barely listening. I just stare into his eyes, enjoying the spark of enjoyment in them. He's just that much cuter when he smiles. It reminds me of our childhood together.

"Look Landon, I've got to go," I interrupt him. He pauses, mid-sentence. His hair flies wildly around his forehead, his eyes peeking through the thin strands.

"We just got here," he says, his voice full of utter confusion. He should have made it here quicker considering the size of his legs. The fact that he didn't make me his main priority upsets me. Sure, I should be grateful for his presence, but he's my best friend.

"*You*, just got here. I've been here for twenty minutes," I imply. Landon swallows, obviously understanding my reasoning. Gently, he wipes his hair from his eyes.

"And anyway, I've got my first date today," I add, trying to perk up. Step one of getting over Landon. I watch his face fall slightly, his lips drooping at the corners. He licks his lips slightly, then tilts his head.

"Cyrus?" He guesses.

I nod. Cyrus has been extremely polite, and is also really smart. He's a good listener, and some things we have in common. Problem is, he isn't Landon, and his company doesn't give me butterflies like Landon's does.

Still, even though I've only seen him one brief time after Landon's party, he seems like a pretty decent guy.

But I refuse to let dad know that he chose well.

"What's he like?" Landon asks. He doesn't look interested at all. Cautious if anything. Part of me wants to brag, but Landon's my best friend, and I'm not that type of person.

"Honestly, he's smart and kind. The only problem is, is that I'm still figuring out if I could possible mate him in the future. People say you can feel it if someone is right for you. I haven't felt anything like that yet-"

"Althea!"

I'm cut off by someone's voice behind me. Landon gazes over my shoulder, and I can see him internally brooding about something. He doesn't look awfully pleased. An Alpha isn't someone you want to make angry, so I'm curious to see who's grinded his gears.

I look over my shoulder, to see Cyrus, wading his way through the grass. He doesn't look pleased at his current adventure, as if he's ruining a new pair of shoes, which is what I suspect is the case. He's carrying a sun-bleached wicker basket, and is dressed in a button up shirt and jeans. He looks quite formal for someone battling through weeds.

He smiles when he sees me, his dark blue eyes lighting up. He stumbles a bit, but recovers. I stand slowly, meeting his gaze. He opens his arms, and engulfs me in a hug. He smells of baked bread for some reason.

I can't tell of I'm excited for this date or not. I *do* want to see if I can get over Landon, and he's not a bad guy to go with. From the Wisdom Pack, he's smart, and knows his manners. His looks are an added bonus, but my mind doesn't stray to far on that note.

"Hey," I respond to his greeting he had mumbled in my ear. I pull away slowly, feeling Landon's penetrating gaze on my back. He's sizing up Cyrus when I turn around.

I get that Landon is going to be protective, I mean I'm his best friend. But if Landon is going to death stare Cyrus for the rest of eternity, I'm not sure this is going to work.

Cyrus seems nervous, as he picks up the basket he had set down to hug me. He nods his head at Landon as a form of respect. For a moment I'm confused, till I realise that we are in the presence of an Alpha, even if it doesn't feel like it.

Okay, maybe it does by the long stretch of silence Landon is feeding like a fire, by just staring at the offered hand Cyrus is showing. I sigh in relief when Landon finally shakes it, not taking his dark brown eyes off Cyrus's wide, scared blue ones.

"I didn't expect to find you here Alpha, *with my date*," Cyrus declares cynically. Landon's jaw clenches in immediate response, and I want to slam my face into my hand.

"Didn't she tell you? We spend *a lot* of time together," Landon states, his voice firm. I Swallow anxiously. I've never seen Cyrus like this. Sticking up for himself doesn't seem like something in his nature. Obviously, it's a common thing involved with an Alpha's nature, especially considering Landon's attitude right now.

"Did she tell you we are going on a date?"

Cyrus holds up the basket for emphasis.

"I'm glad you two met, but it looks like it's time for Cyrus and us to go. See you later Landon?"

Landon tears his gaze from Cyrus, and curtly nods at me. I watch him leave unsure of if he will come back tomorrow morning, or if I won't see him for another week.

***

I watch Cyrus lay the patterned blanket down, and attempt to smooth out the creases. He then places the basket down, and pats the spot next to him. We are perched on the tip of a hill for our date.

It's a pretty awesome setting. We can see the sun illuminate the whole of the Power Pack. It's a pretty massive Pack.

I can see the two different schools, market places and Landon's home far off in the distance.

I take a seat, smiling at Cyrus.

"Thanks for this," I say softly. He runs a hand through his hair, and nods. He brings up a random conversation topic, and we discuss it for some time, as he pulls out sandwiches from the basket. I'm not really hungry. I was till Landon and Cyrus's first meeting.

You could throw water between them and it would freeze.

"Something on your mind?" Cyrus asks, startling me. I had been staring at Landon's house intently, wondering exactly what he was up to. Cyrus warm hand brushes hair from my face. He's awfully close, his thigh brushing against mine.

15

"Nothing," I dismiss, giving him my best smile. How am I supposed to get over Landon when I can't stop thinking about him, even when Cyrus's soft lips are on mine.

I just wish Cyrus was easier to hate.

Chapter Four

"Today was... fun," Cyrus breathed gently in my ear, before moving down to lay his lips on mine. I kissed him back, mirroring his actions. Lunch couldn't have gone any better. I had learnt so much more about Cyrus; how he works, his interests and disinterests.

Everything about him was *almost* perfect. He was courteous, sweet, kind and smart, but there was something about him that didn't fit me, that didn't seem like my mate material.

"We should do it again," I offer, pulling away to smile at him. He smiles back, his lips finding mine again. I tangle my fingers through his thick black hair. His tender approach to loving was an attractive trait for him to have, making it easier to along with, but harder to resist.

After our seemingly successful date, we had walked back hand and hand through the haze of the setting sun. It was rather sweet of Cyrus to walk me to my door.

Suddenly the door pops open, making Cyrus pull away from me in a fright, smooth his shirt out and fold his hands together. I glare toward the door, immediately expecting Dad.

He's happy about Cyrus and I, obviously. But any chance for him weasel his way into our relationship and make sure everything goes to plan would be taken. He probably saw us walk up the driveway and was ready to jump in at the right moment.

But there stood Landon. Hair slicked back neatly, dressed to impress, and he even smelt as irresistible as he looks; like spice and roses. I'm briefly taken aback by him.

Last time I laid eyes on him in my house, he was being chased out the door by my father who welded a wooden spoon. Now there was no incriminating man beside him, bashing him over the head.

He was glaring at Cyrus with some unknown emotion swirling in his light brown eyes. His fists we clenched, and he seemed to look more intimidating with every breath of a moment that past.

"Landon?" His name comes out of my mouth before I can stop it. No matter how hard we had tried to convince my father in the past, he would *not* be swayed on his views about Landon.

"What are you doing here?" I question, gazing at him. He draws his eyes off Cyrus, who fidgets nervously. I take his hand before I can think, enclosing my fingers around his palm.

Suddenly my father appears behind Landon, a massive smile on his face. He surges past him, engulfing Cyrus in a semblance of a *manly* hug, giving him friendly slap on the back. I roll my eyes. It's like father is dating him not me. I still don't understand what or how he came to meet Cyrus in the first place. Although *apparently,* he's my father's workmates son.

If that makes sense.

"Nice to see you. Staying for dinner?" dad asks Cyrus. I can see in his eyes that father desperately wants Cyrus to stay, so he can question him about our date, because he knows I'll be reluctant to tell him. Cyrus sighs.

"Sorry Sir, I've got to make dinner for my mother tonight. Thanks for the offer," Cyrus excuses himself politely. Dad looks ultimately disappointed, but doesn't say anything. Cyrus kisses my forehead gently, then leans in whisper in my ear.

"Don't let Landon get to you," he says so quietly, I almost didn't quite catch it. I glance at him pull away in confusion. Get to me? Cyrus squeezes my hand, winks and walks off down the path. We all watch him go. I glance at Landon quickly, hoping he hadn't heard what Cyrus had just said. Not that I knew exactly what he was talking about.

"Well come on in Althea, Landon is staying for dinner," Dad says with excitement. I blink. Am I hearing, right? I follow them inside, ready to question them profusely. I had to know exactly what Landon had said or done to convince my father.

The house in enveloped in warmth, and something smells delightful coming from the kitchen. I stop Landon by grabbing his arm before when could follow dad into the dining room. He looks at me in confusion, shaking his head.

"How?" I hiss quietly. I'm annoyed he didn't tell me especially if he was planning this. Shouldn't he be off doing productive things, like Alpha work? Instead of scaring my date off who I knew would have stayed if there wasn't an Alpha hanging around the house, romancing my damn father. This is no way to get over him as quick as I hoped.

"We talked," he stated, barely explaining. I want to question him further, make him elaborate, but he pushes past and into the dining room. I follow behind meekly.

Father is already sitting at the head of the table, discussing something with my mother, who holds a plate of roast chicken. My bet is they are talking about Cyrus and me. My hopes are they aren't thinking of setting us up for mating this early.

"Sit, dinner is ready," mother demands softly, briskly walking over to lay a kiss on my cheek. Landon sits in front of where I usually sit for dinner every night. His swirling emerald eyes don't move off me, even when mother bends over his shoulder to deposit a plate of vegetables onto the table.

"So, did you enjoy your date?" Landon asks, tilting his head. I can feel Dad start to listen in curiosity, which makes me bite back the snide remark I had ready for Landon. Landon sweeps his hair back with his hands, and my eyes sweep over his muscular arms I can see under his shirt.

"It was great. He's very...attentive," I muse, forking a piece of chicken onto my plate. Landon doesn't react, just stares and doesn't respond.

"I'm glad you two are getting on. He's the perfect man for you to-"

"Mate?" I cut him off.

He nodded, smiling.

"Don't you think it's a little, I don't know, early to be thinking about mating someone you just met?" Landon questions randomly, getting everyone's attention, even mother, who I thought was too engrossed in stirring the gravy she made.

I glare at him. He knows quite well about how I feel about my father's random pairings. He wants me to admit it.

"You're right Landon, but I actually think you should stay out of it," I snap. I didn't mean for it to come out like it had. Maybe I'm just mad at him for being him; so damn perfect.

He drops his cutlery, his jaw clenching. Why is he so mad? He never shows interest in me at all, so why is he acting so sassy toward the fact that maybe, just *maybe* I found someone who may be good for me. Even if I was having the hardest time getting over Landon.

"Well I'm overjoyed that I picked such a nice man for you Althea," Dad cuts in, his voice happy and bubbly. I tear my gaze from Landon so our death staring match is cut short.

"He is a nice man, too good for me," I mutter. I want to get over Landon, more than anything. But right now, father's interference makes me want to crush my own head in.

19

"Don't say that honey. Cyrus really does like you. I'm sure you will be mated to him soon," Father stated happily. I could tell it was directed at Landon. Landon may have convinced father, but that was my father's way of telling him to back off. This is family business.

"What if she isn't ready to mate *him*?" Landon questions further. I kick his legs from under the table. The quicker the grandchildren come, the better. Father is very evolved in this subject, and becomes exceptionally tense when his opinion doesn't fit everyone else's.

"She will be. It is essential she mates someone proper," dad says back calmly. I nervously watch Landon and father, who don't seem to be meeting eye to eye on this. I don't want father to kick the Alpha out of his house. He may have been a match for Landon before, but now Landon is much stronger and younger.

"And what would you consider, proper?" Landon dares ask. Here we go...

"A man who will pay full attention to her when it's needed, not someone who has other business that always needs tending to," he responds. Landon gently pushes his chair back, and I can tell that both males in the room are beyond pissed. I glance at mother, who busies herself by stuffing chicken into her mouth.

We both know what Alpha's can get like...

"You should consider the fact that she should be with someone she has loved for longer than a week," Landon argued carefully. I bite my lip, trying to catch his gaze. He wants what is best for me. I can tell that.

Father stands as Landon does.

"So what, you think you would be mate material for my daughter? Don't be ridiculous," Father spat. He was getting offensive rather than defensive now.

Landon stands up a little taller, trying to intimidate my father.

"I would do a much better job of caring for her than you..."

Okay, it stops here.

"Stop, both of you!" I shout, rocking the room into silence. Frustrated tears are pushing at the back of my eyes, but before they can I back from the room. I can't deal with either of them right now.

I sprint up the stairs and I hear Landon follow closely behind.

Chapter Five

I stumble up the final step, and push open my bedroom door. The confines of my room are cold, due to the partly open window. Everything is messy for some reason, which I guess was caused by the wind. I'm generally a tidy person.

I turn and shove the door shut, but it catches on something. Annoyed, I grab my underwear and toss them behind me. Trust mother to clean clothes and leave them lying around my room at random. I lean my back against the door, taking a deep breath.

I hear Landon make it to the top of the stairs with ease, and although I climb them every day, I'm breathing heavily.

"Al?"

I close my eyes as Landon's soothing, empathetic voice floats under the crevice of door. It had an immediate, calming effect on me, making me slump and relax against the door. He may have shown up and terrorise my family at this seemingly crucial time, but I couldn't help but admire his company.

"Yeah?" I breathe, blowing a stray lock of black hair from my face. I'm glad I can't see his swirling, distracting dark eyes that make my heart melt *every* time. I hear him tap his finger rhythmically against the door.

Those eyes are his secret weapon against me. He may be the Alpha of the Power Pack, an extremely feared and influential Pack, but his muscles are not the most unnerving weapon he can wield against me.

"Are you going to let me in?" Landon asked gently. I turn and rest my head against the door. Should I? The butterflies flutter in my stomach, just at the thought. I roll my eyes at myself, glad Landon can't see me right now.

I glance over my shoulder to see the black, lacey underwear laying close to my pillow on my bed. Slowly I stalk away from the door, and shove them under the covers, before walking back to the door, wiped my eyes and flinging it open bravely.

21

Landon stood there, looking meekly down at me. Nonetheless, he still looked damn good looking, and suited the look of a white button up shirt and black jeans. He gazed at me, hands shoved in his pockets, eyes glowing dangerously.

I sucked in a deep breath, and without words, walked away and sat squarely on my bed. Landon unsure followed with quiet footsteps. If he wanted to follow I had given him access, and I wondered briefly if this new Alpha power wiped away his awkwardly shyness I loved about him.

This has to be the first time Landon and I have ever been in a bedroom, alone together. For this long, we have been yearning for something like this, or at least I have. The bed creaks as he sits next to me, his gaze meeting mine.

"I want you to know, the I understand *exactly* what you are going through," Landon said softly. My eyes burned at his words, and I fought to cage my tears in. He's right. He does understand, and maybe I shouldn't be the frustrated and upset one...

"At least your family has a reason. They want a proper Luna, a capable guardian for the Pack, who sums Power up as much as you do," I said, my voice awfully dry and hoarse. I shouldn't be mad at him, but for whatever reason, I was on edge.

I jump slightly as Landon grasped my hand. It makes me strangely happy when he does it like; like he's my lifeline that I cling to for support.

"Everything will be okay...Listen to me when I say this; you should pursue the man you *want* to be with, or woman for that matter! Do not listen to what your parents demand, or your friends...this is your choice," he comments. I gaze at him, wondering how he managed to be so sweet for a moment.

"Inspirational," I tease, giving his shoulder a bump with mine. He chuckles, and a friendly mood floods into the room like a wave. He smiles brightly at me, catching my slight hint at a joke. But still, even his beautiful smile can only bring a shred of happiness.

"But seriously. I know that you keep to yourself, so if you ever want to talk about who you *really* want, then I am your guy," Landon stated proudly. Oh great, the whole 'shoulder to cry on' fiasco.

I pause. How are you supposed to spill the truth to your best friend that you've had a crush on him for your whole childhood, and that you hate how this change has separated the two of you, and that him being your mate would exceed your wildest dreams?

I take an internal deeper breath...No way is that happening, unless I know he likes me back somehow.

"I can't see myself be incredibly happy with Cyrus," I admit. I feel bad about it; I mean, he's such a decent guy too. Landon doesn't seem surprised at my answer at all, but he squeezes my hand anyway.

"Yet still, you remain wanting to be with him?"

I could tell Landon was disapproving, but how could I explain to him the basic truth. I stood up, and began pacing, twirling my finger around a lock of my hair nervously.

"There is a difference between wanting, and *needing,*" I stated in frustration, throwing my hands up. Landon just watches me with a curious look on his face.

"Do you feel something for someone else?" He questions intrusively. I come to a rigid stop, my feet skidding against the carpet. I slowly turn my head away, and squeeze my eyes shut...did he really ask that?

"I-I don't know," I stutter unintentionally, placing my hands on my hips. Landon smiles softly, waiting for my answer. My stomach flips at the thought of him maybe actually knowing I like him, or at least have done for years now.

"Yes, you do...come on tell me or I'll stay here all night," he says persistently. I watch him get up, and pull my covers back like he was about to get in, but something stops him. Slowly he turned around, a devilish grin on his face.

I gasp, seeing that clutched in his hand was my underwear. I jumped forward, but he held the pair above my head, making me jump for them.

"Landon," I growled, trying to snatch them from his hands, but he moved back just in time, so I smacked my head against his chest. He laughed loudly, watching my struggles.

"Oh Al, aren't these a little *too* sexy?" He suggested. I backed away, fuming. I wanted to slap him, but I doubt I'll get my underwear back of I even dear. He continued to gaze at me, daring me to come closer again and retrieve them.

"We aren't five, *Alpha,*" I admonished, folding my arms. I wanted him to act more like his age at this point, not like a horney pubescent boy. Okay maybe he didn't completely resemble that; he looked more like a walking Sex God.

"Come get them," he dared, lowering his arm to a point where I could actually grab them. I eyed him carefully, then glanced at the door. He followed my gaze, and I took the chance to lurch forward and grab the underwear. Except his grip wouldn't loosen, even though I had taken him by surprise.

We wrestled for a while, him single-handedly, me with two hands. After a few moments, I was out of breath, struggling.

"Calm down and I'll let you have it," Landon said smoothly, not even worried about the fight for my dignity and underwear. I growled, but stopped.

I gazed up at Landon, who slowly released the underwear. I let them drop to the floor.

"Think of it as a lesson in life. You won't get what you want if you fuss and worry, dear," Landon stated. I gaped at him in disbelief. He was hinting at my parents, and how we had a long-winded argument. He chuckles at my frown.

"You're so cute Al," he commented, pinching my cheek. Suddenly the mood in the room changed, and I felt my gaze graze over his lips, unintentionally. We stared at me, and in that moment, I was almost *sure* that he had started to lean in.

"We are so sorry darling-"

I groan as mother bursts into the room. Of course, why didn't I expect that...

Chapter Six

I stared straight into his deep blue eyes in wonder. They were so clear and pure, with no imperfections or specs in them at all.

Blushing red roses lay on the table in front of me, wrapped in purple coloured cellophane, with a ribbon strung around it. They were wilting already in the heat, dropping down over my fingers as I fondled the petals gently. It was such a nice gesture. They vivid colours clashed with the blue plaid tablecloth and green placemats.

"Thank you, they are beautiful," I sigh, glancing up at Cyrus. He smiles at me, glad I liked his surprise present. I feel a stab of guilt. He is so eager to please me, and I was still grasping to the fact that I could possibly be worthy of him.

We are sitting near the window of a Café, enjoying iced coffees. The quaint place, decorated with floral patterns and eccentric decor, is full with only an elderly couple, and a lone business man who is discussing something casually with someone over the phone. It was seemingly romantic in some aspects, and felt like we finally had some privacy.

"I'm sorry about the other day," I state blandly. I hadn't meant for Landon to come over, and so obviously scare Cyrus away. He must have been worrying about what had happened that night, especially since I hadn't talked to him for the past three days. I mean, how would you like it if the one you wanted to mate was having dinner with an unmated male, who just so happened to be an Alpha?

I had been too busy dealing with my deranged emotions and clingy parents. I hadn't even met with Landon, who I had hoped hadn't been sitting in *our* field, waiting for us pretentiously. Then again, a taste of his own medicine wouldn't hurt the Alpha himself.

"What exactly happened?" He asks. He fiddles with the gold ring on his index finger. I couldn't tell what the meaning of it was, but it had some pattern engraved into the expensive chemical. Maybe it had his parents' names; I was yet to meet them. I didn't even know if he had any siblings.

"Nothing really, it ended up with a massive agreement," I informed him. I wasn't complaining really. I was annoyed, but Landon has stuck up for me, which I would forever be grateful for. Cyrus seemed curious, but I could see the glint of jealousy in his eyes, which was unnecessary till he knew all the details.

Had Landon intended to kiss me? Did I want him to? I mean I have crushed on him *all* my life, but why now? Why now, when he knows I have finally found someone who *may* like me more than I like him, which never happens.

"About?" he asked meekly. I fiddled with the edge of the tablecloth.

"You, actually."

He blinked.

"He just doesn't agree with this whole, arranged mating business," I explained. At least that's what I thought was his perspective. Sometimes Landon has a different way of thinking and interpretating information. Like the time I told him I was crushing on someone and he blew up at me for being too young. I was fifteen, he was 16.

"What's it to him?"

He was getting agitated now. He was fiddling with his ring and ringing his hands. I watch him clench his jaw nervously. I hope this didn't ruin everything for us.

"He's my friend, and he cares about me, that's all. I'm sorry if he doesn't agree, I mean I didn't for some time," I breath. I subconsciously slip my hand under the table and cross my fingers, silently praying he wouldn't get mad. I hoped he even saw it from my point of view, and had been thinking the same thing initially.

"So, you regret this?" He asks, his voice so monotone, it scared me. *Crap.*

I shake my head, feeling strands of hair slip from my braid. I reach across the table and and grab his fist, which was enclosed around a spoon that he had formerly used to stir his drink. I kept my hand on his, my eyes on him till he let he spoon go, allowing it to clatter onto the covered table.

He sighs out in a rush.

"We should just enjoy each other's company," I state, leaning off my chair and over the table. I didn't care if anyone in the Café was look at this point. I was just about to kiss Cyrus and cancel out all that pointless arguing, when the tinkle of the bell over the front door resounded throughout the small room.

I jumped in surprised, knocking my forehead against Cyrus's, causing him to groan in protest. I sat back, rubbing the point of my skull that got the most impact. It wasn't that it hurt *that* much, it just gave me a fright.

I looked up to see who had caused this. Walking toward us was a young woman wearing some sort of a grey, well-tailored suit. I could have mistaken her for a man, especially with that foul look on her face, and short, slicked back blonde hair.

Apart from that, she had remarkable eyebrows.

She strode over with an obvious confidence that seemed to resonant over the room, grabbing the attention of the elderly couple, who had been recently complaining about the lack of service they had received. The clicking of her black stilettos only ceased as she stood in front of our table, glaring straight into my eyes.

I've never been the personality to hold eye contact anyway. Only unless reasonable, and this woman could not be deemed reasonable. Not with those yellowy, sharp eagle eyes.

"Althea Francess Duvey. I have been assigned to give you this," she said curtly. Her accent was strong, suggesting she did not originate from this Pack. Let me guess, Discipline Pack. I shiver, thinking about The Pack we are *all* secretly afraid of, even Landon told me Alpha Dallas isn't someone you would mess with.

A throat clearing noise is what brought my attention back to the table setting. Cyrus looked awfully uncomfortable, as the woman had moved her penetrating gaze over to my companion.

"Who, what?" I sputter, not quite formulating a proper sentence. Her neck snapped back, startling me.

"A handwritten letter from Alpha Landon," she stated firmly, slamming an envelope onto the table. It had the royal wax seal. Bright red, a picture of a closed fist stamped on it, signifying the Power Pack. I reach out and grab the paper, feeling the glossy, almost shimmery finish.

"Our Alpha would like you to respond immediately, and I have been instructed to remain at your side till you reply. I suggest you do so promptly," she snapped in my ear, suddenly closer to my side of the table. So, she was just another one of Landon's slaves. The way she said *our* Alpha unnerved me.

"Alright then," I breath. With all eyes watching me like a hawk, I peel the envelope open. I feel like it's contents have something incriminating on them. Something that Landon knows will genome in trouble with Cyrus.

Wordlessly, I peel the letter from its confines, and unfold it. To revel five simple, linked words, and one name...

I need to see you.

Landon

He even signed it.

"What's my response supposed to be?" I ask, without even needing to think about it. It was exactly what I knew I was going to say anyway. Cyrus remains silent, maybe brooding deeply in frustration.

"He would evidently like to know if you would accompany him," she said, like I was the dumbest person to walk the face of the Earth. I scrunch the paper up without thinking, and honestly, I enjoyed it thoroughly. I watched her swallow her distain.

"I'm on a date, tell him that," I sass, and Cyrus visibly relaxes. Poor guy, he doesn't want this.

But still, my heart yearns to see him again. I should, I *need* to. But not now...

"Go please. Tell him I do not want to see him," I reply, brushing her off. She looks shocked briefly, but covers it in mask of indifference. I watch her run on her heels, and leave the way she came.

I let out a sigh of relief and slam my head in the table. That is not someone I would associate with on a daily basis.

***

Coat on my back, boots on my feet, I crunch across the gravel. Too bad I'm too inconspicuous for a flashlight, so the moonlight is the only source of visibility I have. I mean, this is the sixth branch of skidded over, and nearly broken my own back.

Having successfully snuck out my bedroom window, with a little help from a tired Missy, I had started my night mission.

Landon had no idea I was coming, and by this time, he will probably be fast asleep. Either that or he's out partying. Doubt it though, he can't have changed that much from the doe eyed, young man I used to know.

I need to talk to him, clear things out. I don't care if I want welcome into his home, especially by his father. I *need* to see him.

I can see the gates in the distance, being the only entrance to Landon's estate. He wanted to see me, well here I am.

But suddenly, something clicks beside me. I am flanked by a forest, making everything more nerve raking. I turn my head, staring out into the depths of the greenery. If I had heard correctly, it sounded like the cocking of a gun.

And I was right.

A sudden rush of noise comes from amongst the trees, a swarm of people dressed in black coming for me in all directions.

"Put your hands up and surrender!"

Chapter Seven

My hands are in the air, lights shining in my face. People are surrounding me, their thick boots crunching against by gravel. Guards... Royal Guards. Landon's Royal Guards for that matter. My heart sinks as I realise I'm in big trouble now.

"Back off," I snap, as someone shoves the muzzle of their gun against my cheek. I want to push the dangerously fatal weapon away from blowing my face in, but doing that will increase the chances. Everything is suddenly quiet, as they assess me. I feel myself shift like a true criminal under their scrutiny.

"Accessing Royal property is punishable by law," someone stated from under their mask, their muffled sounding less intimidating. I could feel Landon's note pressing against my hip. I had tucked it into the waistband of my pants as I left, and now I wanted to grab it and shove it into their faces as proof.

"I've come with an... invitation of sought," I reason. Someone lowers their gun so I can use my hands to grab the slip of paper. Not that one lowering the gun made much of a difference, considering everyone was still tense, fingers posed over the hammer of the gun. I unfold the paper, and splay it on the palm of my hand, so the Guard can see.

It's dark, but he still grabs the paper, and assesses it quietly.

"Obviously forgery. Take her back to the Villa and see what the Alpha wants done with her." My heart skips for a moment, thinking the Alpha remained Landon's Dad, but I was tossed back into the crisp pool of reality too quickly. Landon is going to be shocked when he sees me.

With worded protest, handcuffs binding my hands behind my back, and I'm kicked in the back of the knee to get moving. My leg briefly collapses, but I straighten up. Landon is going to get it when I see him.

Only half a dozen Guards from the many that were there actually accompany me. The walk doesn't seem to be long, but one of them keeps prodding the awkwardly sensitive small of my back, sending shooting pain up my spine, and straight into the back of my neck.

30

Once close enough, I could see the glittering lights surrounding the estate. It really is marvellous, although rather flamboyant for my tastes. The guards waste no time hurrying me along the back. The front door was for guests only.

My blatant reasoning was going unnoticed, so I decide to give up. I want to scream, but the authority these men have over me, or the whole Pack for that matter outweigh everything.

Dragged by my arms, we enter the metal door that is installed into the outside of the building. Inside, it is barely lit at all, but I can make out metal bars along the wall. This is nothing like what I've seen before.

The smell was putrid, and groaning resonated off the walls. Were there people in here? Or were those noises from contained animals?

The ground under me clatters and rumbles, as the men push me violently. Landon had to know about this part of the estate, he can't have just been completely oblivious to it.

A hand suddenly swipes out, like it had merged through the wall. It grabbed my hand, frantically clawing at my skin. I yelped and tried to step back, but the Guards had it covered. They smacked the hand brutally with a batten, the sound sickening. With a yowl, the hand retreats back into the cage, and we continue walking. But still, I want to throw up everywhere. Maybe that would be a worthy distraction.

Instead we stop not too far up.

"You, go alert the Alpha," the man flanking me orders another guard gruffly. I see him nod, before scuttling off further up the tunnel like passage. One of the other four shuffles around with some keys from his belt. I can tell he was struggling through the dim lighting.

Eventually he picks up a silver key, and uses it to unlock one of the cage doors. I can't see the place I was being shoved into, as I fall to the floor. The door clanged shut, sealing my fate. Boy, Landon is going to get it when I see him... Really, *really* get it.

The men leave, but not before hearing my proclaimed profanities. I am on the ground, the dirty, filthy, covered in some slimy substance. I stagger to my feet, to find three concrete walls surrounding me. I could only see through the metal bars, everything else was dark.

"Help," I chant out, stumbling toward the bars. They are rusty against my fingertips. Only pained groans come as an answer.

"What's your business here girly?"

I jumped, and turned around. Someone is behind me, I can hear them, but can't see them. I back up, my feet skidding against the floor. They better not have locked me up with a serial killer. Wolves tend to tilt that way when they have phased.

"Who's there?" I question anxiously, pressing myself up against the bars so hard, I could have merged through them. A gasp as I see the shadowy figure move from the corners and slightly into my view. I can see an outline of them. They seem to be a staggering height compared to me.

"No one special... but you, on the other hand, seem like a bucket of sunshine," they state. Their voice was strangely smooth and calming, considering they are probably about to lash out at me with a Stanley knife at any moment. I just wish I could see this man's face.

"I need to get out of here," I gritted out, turning to shake the bars. They groan at the torment, but refuse to budge. The man chuckled at my useless attempts from behind me, like I'm performing a comical act.

"We all do sweetheart, too bad we are locked in her forever," the man graciously implied. A switch flicked in my brain, and I spun around not caring if my own hair hit me in the face.

"I'm not going to be stuck in this place for the rest of my life. Landon is going to come down here any minute now and save me," I snapped. This seemed to shock the man into a quiet void, but I hardly felt remorse.

"You know the Alpha well, eh?"

"All I know, it that I'm going to kill him next time I see his face," I growl, resting my forehead against the metal. I heard the man's footsteps advancing, but I didn't react till a warm hand slapped against my shoulder and he muttered in my ear...."You're not the only one who wants him dead."

I jump, slapping the skin so hard they instantly retract their hand. I hadn't intended it, but his statement worried me, and so did the powerful chants resonating in agreement around the cells. What would these monsters do if they knew I was closer to Landon then they thought?

"Calm it, pretty lady," the stranger warned. I did, sinking to the ground in defeat. If he comes any closer, I'm going to poke him in the eye anyway....

"You can't see anything, so don't make assumptions. I could be a hideous omega for all you know," I bite back. He grunted. Amused by my sassy attitude, but not phased.

"When you've been in here for as long as I have, your eyes adjust to the darkness," he stated. He sounds mad, frustrated by his situation. I don't blame him; I would be too if I was forced to live here, in such a cramped, cold place.

"How long have you lived here?" I find myself asking curiously. It appealed to me that maybe Landon didn't know what was going on down here, and maybe it was his father fault. His corrupting, manipulative father who has some deep hatred for me...That would be nice.

"I was put in here when I was twelve, so seven years," he informed me. I blink in shock, mentally calculating in my head. I had dropped math the year before I dropped school completely, so I wasn't that great. But I could still calculate the fact that he was nineteen years old.

It frightened me more than if he was a fifty-year-old.

"You're nineteen?" I shriek in disbelief, my voice raising louder than intended. I heard him scoot forward, but I crouched back. I wish there was better light so I could see his face.

"Al?"

I gasp, hearing the urgent, frightened sound of Landon. Instantly it was like someone had poured a warm bucket of water over my chilly skin.

"Landon," I call out, desperate to get his attention, so he could set me free. I feel his footsteps quicken, running toward my cell. I suddenly feel angry with him; just relieved and desperate to get out.

"The name's Kace. I know for sure I'll be seeing you again darling," that chilling, deep voice whispered in my ear before Landon made it to the door of the cell. I flinched, knowing they would have slinked back into the corner.

"Al, I'm so sorry," Landon gushed, the moment he saw me. I could hardly see him, but managed to make out the angst on his face. He unlocked the door, after rustling through hundreds of keys. He swung it open, leaving no boundary between us. Finally...

I jumped forward, throwing myself into Landon's grasp. He was warm and smelt like how I remember. He instantly wrapped his arms around my waist, hugging close to his body. His touch instantly calmed me, which was bad considering I should be deathly mad right now.

"I hate you for doing that to me," I state, leaning away to punch Landon in the chest weakly three times, before stuffing my face back into the crook of his neck. I can feel the guilt flowing off him. But he remains quiet.

I feel tears flood my eyes; this man is going to be the end of me.

Chapter Eight

"Care to explain?"

Landon paced in front of me, a frown etched deep into his features. I only sometimes saw him like this; all unkempt and frazzled. Not to mention his distractingly bare torso and lose fitting pyjama pants.

But that's hardly the major subject that needs to be covered at this point.

I sat in some sort of lounge room. It was quaint, dressed in red velvet features. What was seemingly eye catching was the frame strung on the wall. It was of Landon and I, when we were younger. Mother had taken it, but I don't know how he managed to get his paws on it. But I wondered briefly whether or not his father had asked him to take it down yet.

"There is nothing to explain..." he dismissed, folding his hands over each other, and resting his chin in them while he continued to walk back and forth across the fur rug with his bare feet. I gave him a deadpan look, wishing I could look inside that head of his. Did he seriously think I would dismiss this, and walk home without an explanation? Does he not know me at all?

"Nothing to explain? You won't even tell me why you have underground holding cells?" I question. Having experienced these first hand pushed my frustration to get it into Landon's head. He looked especially pained by this, like he was fighting some sort of eternal war. Don't tell me he's the one dictating this...

"Those cells hold bad people Althea. They are there to stop them hurting people like you," he stated. Damn, he sounded so reasonable right now, and I had no argument to retort back with. I hate it when he uses his logic to overpower anything; it makes me feel inferior to him. But still, I will always be the one to question his judgement.

"So what, someone walks into your 'territory' and all hell breaks loose? You lock them up underground in some filthy cell with a possible serial killer?"

That should do it, or at least I hope it will.

Landon sighs and walks over to where I sit, kneels down. He had allowed me to shower, even in these early hours of the morning, before he demanded some answers to my questions. I was wrapped up in a mink blanket, watching his every dangerous move.

"It was for the Royals' safety... we can't just have *anyone* walk in," he explained. He was giving me *that* look. The look that meant 'shut up and listen to he me Althea, I am the reasonable one here' that I see all too often. It always came back to being the damn Alpha of this joint.

"Am I, anyone?" I asked, sounding pettier than intended. I just wanted Landon to explain to me *why* I had to undergo that. Landon sighed and grabbed my hands between his own, running his fingers across the top of my hand. He seemed troubled, looking straight into my eyes.

"You can come here *whenever* you want," he answered softly. Except when his father is around. Thank God he's probably asleep right now, or else I would have remained in those cells for the rest of the night till either my family, or Cyrus would bail me out.

"I came here to ask you about that note that you wrote," I stated, and he nodded. I was here, in front of him. He had seen me, now what? It made me nervous to think about what was going to be said between us. I didn't want to break our friendship up at the seams, but looking at his face, I see a glimpse of someone different.

"I wanted to invite you to a lunch, later in the week," he exclaimed, taking me by such surprised, I dropped his hands, my eyes widening. A lunch? That's what this is about. You're telling me I was locked up against my will to hear him ask me to lunch?

"Seriously," I question in disbelief. Had I heard wrong? Maybe fatigue is getting to me. What time is it? 3 AM maybe? He looked away, then back at me, nervously. He nodded slowly. I couldn't tell which one of us was the most awkward.

"Yes, I am attending a lunch with the Alpha of the Wisdom Pack, and since you're my friend, I wanted you to accompany me," he explained, giving me a tight smile.

I had heard only rumours about Alpha Alden of the Wisdom Pack. He wasn't feared like some Alpha's, but respected. His Pack was responsible for many technological creations that spread through many Packs. But his intelligence will be intimidating, I can tell already.

"You want me to come all the way to the Wisdom Pack with you?" I had to make sure he *actually* meant it first. You can never tell with an Alpha.

"Yes Althea. Alden insisted I invite you, and since invitations are plus one, I figured you would want to bring someone with *you.* Your father maybe?"

He looked uneasy, knowing I wasn't going to bring my father. Never in a million years. I felt my heart plummet to my feet. Cyrus had been talking about an opportunity to get into the Wisdom Pack. Maybe this was his chance...To talk first hand with the Alpha himself over a lunch.

But would Landon be mad? There's only one way to find out.

"You wouldn't mind if Cyrus comes, right?"

If he's picking up on how nervous I am, wringing my hands together and such, he doesn't show it. He stares at me blankly for a few painful moments, before shrugging carelessly.

"Should I mind?" He asks. I can sense some sort of play on words there, but I don't question too much. He doesn't need to be jealous.

"No... It's just, it doesn't seem like you like him that much," I stutter. He shrugs again. He stands up straight again, turning on his heel to walk out the room. Confused, I stand also, and wander out after him. He was walking down the hallway, toward a flight of stairs.

"Landon, what are you doing?" I question, following him up the stairs. We were having an important conversation, and he decides it about the right time to just leave? Alpha's these days.

He continues to mindlessly lead me up the stairs. I've never really had the guts to wander around his home, so seeing this is new. But still, an uneasy feeling sets in. If his father sees me, I'll be in big trouble for sure. Landon doesn't seem to mind, ambling along carelessly.

"Up here," is all Landon says, pointing weakly to a door right at the end of the corridor. I briefly reminded myself that I *do* trust Landon, and that the fact we are beat friends hasn't changed. Maybe a little, but it's not like he's going to open the door, for me to keep walking and plummet into a pile of snakes or something.

But, he leads the way, opening the door and slipping in. He leaves it open partially, intending for me to follow. And I do so, wondering what game he's playing.

Turns out he has lead me into a bedroom. His bedroom I guess.

He holds the door open for me to enter, watching my every move. Nervously, I amble in. His room is massive compared to even my house. Mainly because of the high ceilings. Although, the walls are bland. Only a few portraits line the wall.

One was of him and his mother, before she passed. The other was of Landon and I when we were younger. I must have been thirteen and still figuring out my feels for Landon.

I turn back around, as I hear the click of the door. Landon stared at me, eyes no longer that warm brown colour I love, but cold and coal black. I have never seen him like this, but I have heard that Alpha's can get angry. This was more unnerving, because I could see the livid anger brewing under his skin.

"You're right Althea," he stated, making me shiver. It's not very often I hear him say my whole name. Al is a nickname he gave me when I was a lot younger. It's stuck since. But now, as I take a step back, I know this isn't friendly.

"I am?"

He nods.

"I hate Cyrus. Because he doesn't deserve to be with you," he proclaimed, his voice deadly soft. I swallowed, feeling my nerves bubble up in my throat. Why is he telling me this now? But I stayed quiet, wanting to hear what he had to say.

"In fact, I don't see why you want to be with him...to mate *him*," Landon spat, utter disgust and distain evident in his voice. I flinched, as he stepped closer. I matched his steps back, needing air to he able to think properly. I could smell his spicy scent from quite the distance already.

"Landon it's fine, *he's* fine," I tried to explain, my voice coming out desperate. Why can't he understand! He stalks forward, as I back up, till my spine hits the wall. I winch, but Landon doesn't take notice, till the tips of his feet touch mine. He looks at me, impassively.

"You can't love him, you need someone who you're more compatible with," he insisted. His arms moved suddenly, his palms slamming against the wall beside my head, his arms locked into place. He leant in, till I could smell his recently mouth-washed breath against my neck. I had my head turned, afraid of what might happen.

"You wouldn't know," I gritted out in frustration. Landon sighed, leaning in further till his soft lips pressed against my neck lightly, briefly, making me gasp. What is he doing?

"Trust me, I know *exactly* who you suit," he whispered. My hands remained pressed firmly against the wall, as I felt unsure of what to do. His words were chilling, leaving me reluctant, but wanting to move my hands to touch him, finally feel what it's like.

"Remember the night at your house after dinner?" He asked, his lips leaving soft kisses up to my ear. I shuddered, nodding. He smiled gently against my skin.

"I *did* want to kiss you."

Chapter Nine

Everything from that moment happened too quickly to register at first.... If I had known there was a bookshelf above my head, maybe I wouldn't have chosen *that* wall to back into.

If the encyclopaedia hadn't toppled from its place above our heads, maybe things would have turned out differently. Maybe Landon wouldn't have snapped out of his trance, and I wouldn't have been left speechless. Perhaps our duties would look different...

But it did. It smacked him right on his forehead, so he stumbled back, completely confused by the turn of events. He now stared at me with eyes a soft brown, no longer dark and threatening.

"Shit, sorry Al," he rushed, as I tried to gather my wits. He *was* about to kiss me, but it looked as if his trance had vanished into thin air. I brushed my hands down my jacket, trying to calm my beating heart. I felt a cold tension build between us. That stupid book had broken the spell between us. It had chosen that one time to free itself from bookshelf above.

"It's okay," I croaked, swallowing. He ran a hand through his hair, making it flop over his eyes slightly. Why did that have to happen, to me? I don't understand why I couldn't just have things uncomplicate themselves so that everything in my life made sense. Landon would finally see through the feelings he could possibly have for me.

"It's just...Ever since I phased, I've been having strange feelings. Dad said it's because I haven't mated with anyone yet," he explained. That made a lot of sense. I felt a sense of pity swirl around my stomach. I don't know why though. Maybe it was the guilt I felt. For the fact that I had nearly kissed Landon straight on the lips, and wouldn't have cared for the consequences in that brief moment.

"I see. I understand Landon," I said softly. He smiled at me, but the look in his eyes showed me clearly, that he no longer saw me the way he used too. This sudden change in his attitude had shown him that I was no longer the girl that he had grown up with, and loved like a friend.

I didn't want to admit that things were about to change, but could I push the fact away?

***

"You what! He what?"

Missy sat across from me lounging on my couch. She looked appalled, but excited at the same time. Usually she's not too interested in what I've got to say most of the time. That's what bugs me, but it looks like this has piqued his interest highly. She pulled herself up into sitting position.

I got back earlier this morning. I had convinced Landon I couldn't stay the night because my parents would kill me. That is actually true, but so is the fact that I wanted to leave before his father awoke. I had spent the next day pretending I was ill.

Mother fretted, Dad left for work, and eventually mother followed suit. It's not that their company isn't nice, it's just I needed time to think. But it felt like I was digging myself deeper into a dark trench. I even text Cyrus saying I was going to sleep my sickness off for the rest of the day.

It felt stupid to lie to him, but I didn't want to drag him into this. He said it was okay, and that he was going to go golfing with his Dad anyway. So, I called Missy.

I hadn't talked to her in ages, and it seemed as though her optimistic attitude would cheer me up immensely. So, she agrees, cancelling a day of gardening with her Mum to come over and listen to me vent. That makes me feel instantly better.

"I know, it was as if he was in a trance," I explained, running my hand down my face. Missy thought for a moment, before bending over to the coffee-table to grab a handful of salt and vinegar chips from the bowl I had prepared for her. She shoved on in her mouth and chewed noisily. I knew those chips were her favourite, but the way she ate them wasn't *my* favourite way, that's for sure.

"A trance? You think he *actually* meant to.... you know, kiss you?"

I threw my hands up. How would I know? Landon and I had been best friends for years. How could he possibly known I had feelings for him when I am too shy to tell him anything. Missy seemed to read my expression.

"Think of it this way...Why would he be triggered to attack you like that when he doesn't like you? Does he not have to have some sort of attraction," she questioned. I could see how her could be possibly realistic. I breathed in

40

deeply. I was stuck for ideas, and I could hear my phone buzzing in my pocket. Cyrus obviously wanted to know how I was.

"Maybe I should concentrate on Cyrus," I queried. Missy dismissed this instantly, like she does with many things. A finely manicured finger pointed straight at me, and I felt slightly nervous by the look on her face. He statements left me with a little bit of hope though.

Ever since Missy and I began to tolerate each other's presence, she knew about Landon. I had turned down a boy she thought was good for me. I had to explain to her that I wasn't interested in *him*, which sparked a massive debacle, which might I say has been pestering me for years now.

Now she is obsessed with us becoming mates. It hardly makes sense, but sometimes she tells me it's because she doesn't have a mate. It won't be too far away that she will find one. She pretty, tall and charismatic. I could learn a few things from her confident attitude.

"No, you and Landon have obvious chemistry. If he isn't completely aware, it's a subconscious crush he has for you. Heck, he probably loves you," she affirmed. I rolled my eyes. Loves me? That's a little too far.

"You ask him for his opinion yourself then, if you're so desperate to know whether he likes me or not," I challenge. Missy screws her nose up. Confrontation, she doesn't like the sound of that.

Suddenly a knock another door scares me to jumping position. I glance at the clock, seeing the time was exactly three in the afternoon. My parents weren't to be home for a while yet, so my guess flew out the window. Missy looked panicked, like she was caught red handed.

"Who is that?" Missy questions. I place my finger to my lips, and creep to the window. If I get the right angle without breaking my neck, I'll be able to see who is loitering outside my door.

Cyrus, standing with a bouquet of flowers in his hands. I ducked, glancing at Missy. She stared at me in confusion for a moment, before following suit, crouching in an awkward position in the other side of the coffee-table.

"It's Cyrus, he can't know you're over," I snap. Missy's eyes widen in fright. For a few moments, I watch her get up and run in circles, wondering what to do. Great, now Cyrus is going to find out that I've had Missy over the whole day instead of him. Sometimes a girl needs another girl...

"You've got to leave through my bedroom window!" I exclaim. She pauses, breathing heavily. She looks utterly disgusted by my idea. Maybe because the drop from my window isn't the shortest distance.

"I am *not* jump-"

"You've got too, I'll be dead otherwise," I hiss.

"He isn't your Dad!"

"And!"

"Althea, are you in there?" Cyrus's intrusive voice cuts through our tense argument. Missy sighs in frustration.

"Fine, but you owe me," she growled, turning and trotting up the stairs. I should probably tell her how much I love her, but I'll do that later. I mentally make a note to do so, as I open the front door.

"Hey Sweetheart, how are you feeling?"

I let out a deep breath, and stepped out to give Cyrus a hug. He was dressed to impress, which was surprising because he had just come to see me, who he thinks is utterly sick. It did feel nice to have his comfort again though, but something made my stomach turn and plummet to my feet.

"Why do you smell like perfume?" I question. I watch his eyes fill with some emotion I couldn't decipher; yet it still stirred annoyance inside me. We were surely a thing now, right?

Landon played at the back of my mind though. No, it didn't happen, and even if it did, Cyrus would be the first person I would tell. Mainly because of guilt, and the fact that I do respect him. But it looked like whatever he was keeping from what not about to come out.

"It's the flowers," he excused, pushing them at me. I took them from him. They were ornamental, they didn't smell. He probably didn't realise, so I set them down on the stand beside the door. I felt a bit sick to my stomach. I probably deserved it.

"How was golf?" I asked, stepping aside to let him in. Did he even go? I wanted to ask, bur I felt like it would seem like I was accusing him. I honestly didn't want him to think that, especially if he wasn't doing anything bad.

"Golf...Oh yeah it was great," he commented. I nodded. I sat down on the couch, letting him sit down beside me. I could feel the tension, but it was as though he couldn't, as he lay a warm hand on my thigh. I glanced at him, to see him staring blatantly at my lips.

"Are you feeling any better?" He asked quietly. I swallowed, nodding. His hands traced slight circles around my inner thigh, making me shiver. He leaned, till his breath was mingling with mine. This felt wrong.

"But my stomach is still queasy," I stated loudly, breaking the trance between us. He blinked, leaning back. Good, it worked...

"I actually wanted to ask you something," I continued, feeling how out of place he felt on my father's leather couch, which he worships. He nodded for me to ask.

"Landon invited me to a dinner at the Wisdom Pack, and I was wondering whether or not you wanted to go."

His eyes lit up, so blue and fresh. I smiled as he stood up, looking more excited than a kid on Christmas day. He grabbed my hands, kneeling in between my legs.

"Of course, thank you!"

I was right, knowing that he did want to meet this Alpha. Would he leave though? Would expect me to come with him?

I couldn't imagine a life like that. Without Landon.

Chapter Ten

"You're sure?"

I nod, pushing the pin further into my hair, watching it disappear into my black tresses. I feel Cyrus's eyes on me, as I wipe a bit of smudged lip gloss off my chin. I slowly sit back into my seat, flipping the sun visor and mirror back up into its place above my head.

"It will be fine, can you drive already?" I sigh. Cyrus pauses, before turning the ignition on again. We were meeting Landon at his estate, where we planned to drive him to the Wisdom Pack. He would probably refuse, saying he had a driver already or something. Oh well, I didn't want to walk here, not with the storm that had rolled in.

Cyrus had nervously parked outside the gates of Landon's personal Territory. Last time I was here, I was being dragged to captivity against my will. He wanted to make sure he *really* had been invited. I know, I couldn't believe we were about to meet another Alpha. Some weren't even lucky to meet one at that.

The window wipers moving in a blur in front of my eyes made me feel slightly nauseas, but I didn't say anything. I wasn't completely certain about those flowers, and the perfume, if it even was perfume.

I had dressed as well as I could. I'm not used to dressing up that often, so my mother's old dress I borrowed felt wrong. It was itchy and tight around my waist; which I didn't feel overly confident, mainly because I'm sure I've gained weight lately. But this was a too special of an occasion to where my normal drab.

Once we had been let in through the over strained protection unit, known as Landon's Guards, we ventured inward. Cyrus drove slow, painfully slow. So slow, I had begun to dig intents in my skin. Once he came to a stop, all original drive flew out the window. I sat hopeless in my seat for a few moments.

I stared out the window, dotted with raindrops, to Landon's front door.

"Are you okay?" Cyrus asks intrusively. He leans over and grabs my hand off my lap, cradling it softly in his own. It didn't do anything to quell my nerves.

"I'm fine," I mutter, giving him a soft smile. He nods, and opens his door, stepping out. He doesn't seem too fazed by the fact that the rain was pouring down around him, flatting his hair over his forehead. Maybe it is because he is fixated on that fact that the front door of the Landon's home cracks open. We both watch curiously, as Landon walks out, holding hands with some girl.

My mouth instantly falls open. Who the heck is that?

"Hey guys, you're early!"

I continued to stare blatantly, not really aware of my actions. She stared straight back at me, with eyes so black I swear I could myself in them. I hadn't even gotten out of the car yet. Landon and the girl watch me slowly make my way from the car, cringing ad the rain immediately began to soak through my dress. Once again, I ignored Landon's gaze, finding myself attracted to *her* dangerous gaze.

It felt she was talking to me, like she was transferring her own thoughts into my mind. Something about her, had an unfamiliar, unpleasant aura that surrounded her, which left a foul taste in my mouth.

"Yeah, we thought we could beat the rain, but I guess not," Cyrus replied blandly, snapping my trance away, so I could concentrate on reality. I could still feel the girl staring, but I remained transfixed on a pot plant outside their front door.

Cyrus looked at me, motioning for me to come under the shelter, that Landon and the girl huddled under. They were both dressed remarkably nice, and her long brunette waves were perfectly in place. I grit my teeth, trying not to be jealous, as I feel my hair expanding on my head from the growing humidity.

I take Cyrus's hand and step up the stairs, coming to a stand beside Landon. His smart suit gave me a sudden urge to run my hands down his chest.

"Oh, then is Natasha. She is coming with us," Landon said, finally addressing the woman by his side, who clutched to his side like a lost child. I wasn't angered by her presence, just curious.

"Althea," I stated, smiling a little. Hopefully this front won't wear off later tonight. She stared at me, not smiling. Awkwardly, I lowered my gaze to my shoes, which were getting dotted in raindrops. I felt Cyrus place his hand on the small of my back gently.

"I have our car, if you want us to take you," Cyrus offered politely. I could tell he was nervous, especially in front of the Alpha. His hand shook slightly on my back. I guessed he wanted to come off generous, so that Landon didn't think he was using him. At least that's what I hoped he was doing.

"Sure thing," Landon answered, giving us all a big smile. He didn't look at me. I was briefly surprised at his acceptance, as usually it is hard for him to receive things. Maybe it had something to do with Natasha.

I hung back, as Cyrus reopened the car doors.

Apparently, Natasha got car sick easily, so she took front seat so she could watch the road, while Cyrus took the driver's side. I was now stuck in the back, with a well-dressed Alpha, that was in an all too pleasant mood. He even smelt familiar, which let me relax back into the soft interior of Cyrus prized car.

"How are you?" Landon asks softly, once we had hit the road. It was a good three hour drive to our Neighbouring Pack. All the Packs were formed in a circle, each claiming a set of land to themselves. Purity Pack is the furthest from the Power Pack.

"Natasha? Who is *she*?" I question, my voice a hushed whisper. Luckily, the radio is turned up, so we can listen to Purity Pack news reporters through the static. Landon scoots a bit closer, watching me.

"A friend," he answers, looking back out the window. I think about that. It *has* to be a recent thing, considering the fact that his father didn't like him being 'friends' with girls. Then again, dis his father like anything?

"She's not all that talkative," I note, glancing at the back of the headrest. I can see her light brown hair peeking through. Strangely, I see many familiarities between Landon and Natasha, who's face, which I saw through the side mirror, was still as completely impassive.

"She's shy...nervous," Landon excuses weakly, looking back at me.

"I get that, I do. What made you decide to bring her?" I asked quietly. I had nothing against her presence. It was mainly the fact that he had invited me, when he could have invited her.

"I'm trying to make an impression. She's Alpha Axel of the Passion Packs sister. I hurt her, he will personally snap my neck," he whispers back. Oh...So this was a planned Alpha agreement?

"So, you're using her?" I question. His face contorts in disgust, like he can't believe what I'm even insinuating. He glances at Natasha to make sure she didn't hear what I had just said.

"No, I'm not. Look, it's hard for me. I'm mateless, and I can't run a Pack on my own. It's getting harder for me to control myself," he explained lowly. I understand that Alpha's need a mate more than normal Wolves, like me.

"And there isn't anyone else?"

Landon stared at me blankly for a moment.

"No Al. I mean it's easy for you, you have Cyrus," he exclaimed. I saw Cyrus's eyes shift to the rear-view mirror as he heard his name. Within no time, he went back to shifting through radio stations.

"Yeah...But lately things have been, *weird*," I say so softly I'm not sure if my words got lost within the sound of the loud exhaust. Landon looks interested in this.

"Weird, how?"

"I don't know, he just been a little bit different. I feel like maybe I am with him just to help him. Like getting into the Wisdom Pack, which is his goal. I just sometimes wonder what will happen after that."

"You won't go with him, will you?" He asks, sounding panicked. He grabs my hands, squeezing them tightly till I wince.

"I-"

"What way is it again? Left, or right?"

Cyrus says, seemingly confused, as we come to an intersection. The lack of signs didn't help the situation. Landon pus away, so my hands fall on my lap, still tingling from his touch. He looks out the window.

"Left," he answers. The moment was gone, and when Landon turned back, he didn't question me further. Good, because I didn't know the answer to his question.

We drive in silence, once Landon had given up on a working channel that didn't include the radio presenters voice laced with static. But every now and again, Cyrus would ask for directions, which Landon would provide.

By the time we had gotten there, having driven through the cold depths of the world outside Pack walls, and having entered the Wisdom Packs gates, my legs were cramped beyond belief. The whole time I wanted to lean into Landon, but I refrained.

Eventually though, we *were* there. Wisdom Pack was a lot more developed and intricate compared to my Pack. Poverty hardly touched any areas.

Alpha Alden's home was quite the spectacle. And I thought Landon's home was something you could only see in dreams. It hardly compared to anything I had seen beforehand.

47

We pulled up somewhere near the front, after being escorted by what looked like Guards. Cyrus and I were ultimately in awe, Cyrus nearly crashing the bonnet through the gardens. Landon didn't seem fazed, and nor did Natasha.

"Come along. He will be waiting," Landon instructed, popping the door open and stepping out carelessly. A small man scuttled down the stairs from the front door quickly. But Landon dismissed him. It probably looked confusing, considering the Alpha of the Power Pack had showed up in a beaten up old Corolla.

He rounds the car and open the door for Natasha, who elegantly steps out onto the stones, while I stumble out on my own accord.

The air was warmer here. The humid air clung to my skin possessively, and I found it increasingly hard to swallow.

"Friends, come on in, I have air conditioning," a voice called up from the top of the stairs. We all looked up, seeing a man, with folded arms, gazing down at us.

"Alden, how good to see you," Landon greeted warmly, as if they were the best buddies. This was probably true. Landon trotted up the stairs, with Natasha trailing along behind. Him and Alden shook hands, greeting each other. Cyrus and I followed up, unsure of what to do.

Alpha Alden turned to me, giving me a warm smile, that instantly relaxed my nerves. He held out his hand, which I took. I met his dark blue gaze for a brief, compelling moment.

"Alpha Alden, Wisdom Pack. You must be Althea."

Chapter Eleven

Alpha Alden was extremely hospitable. He graced us with comments often, and his staff offered us food and drinks at every corner. His place was *decked* out with many new gadgets that hadn't even reached the Power Pack.

"Most of these are the original prototypes for some of the best creations Wisdom Pack have made," Alden explains, seeing us all observing a table with unexplainable technology littered on it.

What I found most interesting was the endless number of bookshelves stacked with books that were situated around the strangest places, and all I wanted to do was grab a book and sit down to read. I could tell Cyrus was itching to touch everything he saw.

"This way is the dining room, if you want to have lunch now," Alpha Alden offered, pointing in the direction of the hallway. We all nodded. I noticed Alden held back, whispering something to Landon as we walked in front, but I dismissed is, thinking it was simply Alpha business.

Once we had been seated, Alpha Alden started talking about his Pack. I was sitting next to Landon. For whatever reason, Cyrus wasn't seated next to me, but Landon. Natasha sat opposite me. Alden new something I didn't it seemed...

Landon had just brought up trade deals, when I saw something flicker at the corner of my eye. It was just by the door, like a flash of colour that vanished in a second. I frowned, finding myself to be intrigued by the strange happenings outside the room. Cyrus seemed to notice, catching my eye from across the table.

"You okay?" He mouthed, his dark eyebrows creasing together. Him and Alden were similar, with the same inky hair and strikingly blue eyes. Although Alden carried himself with much more sophistication and grace. You could tell which one was the Alpha out of the two.

I nodded, glancing back to the door.

A pair of the lightest brown eyes were staring through the crack in the door. I gasped, grabbing everyone's attention. Alpha Alden eyes followed my gaze, to see the figure hovering in the door.

"Oh, Melia, come in," Alden instructed, standing up. Melia?

A timid looking girl suddenly emerged through the door, her hands folded in front of her. Her hair was the softest brown colour, like her eyes. She stared at me warily. Did she live here?

"This is my student...I have been teaching Melia personally due to her failed results in the Wisdom Packs tests," Alden explained, pulling a chair back for Melia to sit in. She did so silently.

Tests? Man, I'm glad I don't live here. I glance at Cyrus to see he's unfazed by this. He's smart.

"So, Alden, is Melia your mate?" Natasha asks. Everyone goes silent. That was one of the first times I heard her talk since her complaints about car sickness. But what a strange question to ask.

"No," Melia excuses quickly, going seemingly paler. Alden remains quiet, staring straight at Melia as she swallows awkwardly.

"Why not?" Natasha continues. Man, she's really pursuing this.

"Why are you asking?" I snap. I cover my mouth with my hand in fright, not believing that had come out of my mouth. Great, now the Alpha's probably think low of me for snapping at a girl who was just asking a question. But I mean, it wasn't even her business.

"I was creating conversation, since no one else seems to be too good at it," she replies snarkily. I flinch, my cutlery clattering noisily on my ceramic plate. Alden began to chuckle warmly, whole Cyrus looked petrified by what was going on.

"It's called being polite," I shot back. Natasha frowned, anger glinting off her eyes. I felt a hand on the inside of my thigh, making me jump. It was warm and soothing, and as I looked to my left, I saw it was Landon, who's arm was tucked under the table inconspicuously.

"Calm down," he murmured, glancing at me. His soft brown eyes looked pained, willing me not to argue with his companion.

My dress was short, but luckily covered important areas. Landon's finger tickled around the edges, and I prayed for him to take his hand off me. Not because it didn't feel good, I just felt uncomfortable considering Cyrus was sitting on the other side of him, and Alpha Alden sat vertical to me. Natasha, I didn't care.

"Landon, you should come sit next to me," Natasha offered, patting the seat next to her. Landon's hand froze on my leg. Her voice had turned sickly sweet instantly when addressing Landon, like she was sucking up to her Alpha.

"His food is here," I cut in, before Landon can stand. Natasha ignores me, continuing to smile at Landon, motioning with her head for him to come closer.

This was unnecessary. It was obvious she was staking a claim, ensuring we knew that Landon was with *her*.

"Why doesn't everyone just stay where I seated them," Alden states firmly. I see Natasha bite her lip, staying quiet to his demands. Landon's hand goes back to rhythmically stroking my inner. Irritated, I place my hand over his, beckoning for him to stop.

"So, Althea, do you like the Power Pack?" Alden questions nonchalantly, trying to fill the void of silence that had just coated the room. I looked back from where I was frowning at Landon, who's short nails dug into my thigh.

"I like it there, but-"

"She has ties, that will ensure she stays," Landon cut, smiling so broadly, I was taken aback. Alden raised his eyebrows, nodding in understanding. Cyrus seems slightly bothered, but doesn't say anything. I can tell everyone is suddenly careful about what they say around Alden.

"Understandable. Have you no interest in joining my Pack?" Alden questions. Landon's hand tightens further on my leg, making me wince slightly. I pry at his fingers, feeling my face heat up immensely. I could feel the salad we were eating for lunch churning within my stomach.

"Cyrus has immense interest in becoming a Wisdom Pack member. He's very smart," I say quickly, turning the heat off me. Cyrus's eyes widened, as the attention was suddenly in him. He set his piece of wheat bread back down on his plate nervously. Alden turned in seat, no longer interested in what I was saying.

He began to question him profusely about his intentions.

"You can take your hand off me Landon," I snap, making sure my voice was hushed. Natasha seemed bored anyway, paying more attention to the tree out the window then our conversation. Alden had his arm slung loosely around the back of Melia.

Landon stared down at me, his lips turning up on the side. I found felt his palm burn against my skin. I narrowed my eyes, wishing his own weren't such a captivating green.

"Why? Don't you like it?" He asked, his voice sensually soft. I swallowed, trying not to make a noise, and he begins to move his hand further up, so that it disappears beyond the hem of my dress.

"Landon," I murmur a warning. I can see the edges of his irises begin to darken, which sets off a warning inside me.

I remember him telling me he loses control easily. The sight of his eyes was burned into my head; so dark and soulless. What would happen if he lost control here? He's only a new Alpha.

Alden seemed to notice, looking our way more than once, even as Cyrus chatted away to him.

"I've ways liked the way you say my name," he whispered lowly. I shivered, but didn't answer. Looking back, it was as though the fresh green colour of his eyes was stained black. It was as though slivers of poison was leeching towards his pupils.

"I need to use the bathroom," I exclaim loudly, standing up so that Landon's hand fell back unnoticed. Everyone was silent, watching me. My cheeks were stained red, and I was sweating, making me probably look exactly how I felt; absolutely flustered, with no denying it.

I didn't ask where the bathroom was, I just left the room as quickly as I could. I closed the door behind me, winching when it slammed against the wall, knocking something that was probably worth a lot of money onto the ground.

I let out a deep breath. What was Landon doing? Did he feel as much as a connection with me, as much as I did him?

I shook my head, placing my hand over my beating heart. For moment there, I thought I was dreaming.

Suddenly the door opens just as drastically as I had slammed it.

I jump back defensively. Landon stood there, staring at me with eyes so black, I could see myself in the reflection. I swallowed, as he slowly closed the door behind him. Now what?

"You shouldn't have left Althea," he murmured. I backed a step away nervously, my heart rate accelerating exponentially once again. Was he mad at me for some reason, or was this something else?

"Sorry, I was being touched inappropriately by my Alpha," I snapped, taking another shuddering step backwards. It was stupid to do this; he was enjoying the chase, I could see it in his eyes. But space between us kept my head clear. Landon raised an eyebrow at my words.

"Tell me you didn't like it," he says huskily. This was a different side of him...More primal and erotic. His whole demeanour was intimidating, but I knew I had to hold my own. I went to reply, but nothing came out of my mouth.

I backed slowly, till my back bumped against the wall. Landon's mouth curved into a malicious smile, as he advanced further, till the tips of his shoes were against mine. His hands move to either side of my arms, trapping me in. I leant back as far as the plaster would allow me, wishing I could melt back into the wall.

I could feel his warm breath brushing against my cheek, his nose almost touching mine. I didn't know what to do. Should I duck under his arms and run? No, he would chase me.

"Why are you acting like there isn't something between us," he murmured sensually. I bit my lip, drawing his attention.

"Why are you doing thi-"

I was cut off by his lips touching mine.

I was so taken aback by it, for a second I didn't know what to do. All I could think was that Landon was kissing me... Actually kissing me. That I can't be dreaming, that my hands moving involuntarily up his arms, and to his face was a hallucination.

Everything around us vanished, as I concentrated on Landon's soft lips moving against mine. Every worry flew away, as the moment I had been waiting for finally happened. My hands glided through his soft brown hair, feeling the soft strands brush through my fingers. His tongue tenderly touched mine, while his fingers moved down to my hips.

But it wasn't long before his soft touch changed tact.

He pulled away from my lips, letting me breath, and with a feral need, he continued to leave wet kisses down the side of my neck. My breathing was harsh, as I pulled on Landon hair. He had lost control completely, but so had I.

But what happened next was beyond anything I thought was possible.

Holding my wrists above my head with one of his hands Landon kissed one spot softly, before digging his teeth into my neck. I gasped, trying to wiggle out of his grip. Pain filtered from the bite, and to my head. It was so painful, I briefly convinced myself I was having a brain aneurysm.

Before long, he pied away, his eyes, as black as night, meeting mine again. He had marked me...

"What have you done?"

Chapter Twelve

Blood trailed down my fingers, as I held the wound on my neck. The pain was throbbing and consuming, but I could still feel the surprise pulsing through. Everything was setting in deeply, making me feel utter dread wash across my whole being.

"You marked me," I repeated. Landon's eyes were fading from black, to the pale green they usually were. Blood trickled down his chin, sealing the fact that I no longer belonged to *no one*. He nodded slowly, watching me warily.

He suddenly looked better than before. It was as though I was looking at him through a set of new eyes. Eyes that magnified every contour of his face and body. It marked places that made me feel attraction for him ten times over.

"Why?" I question. It was all I could say. I wanted to be mad at him, but I could feel the bond between us. It was as though I wanted to *confide* in him about my problem, even though he *is* the problem. His arms looked awfully inviting at the moment... But the need to cuddle would have to wait.

"It was necessary," he stated simply. Necessary? Was that all he had to say to me? He wasn't even apologising for the fact that he marked me, without my permission. I pulled my hand away, seeing it covered in blood. At the same time, Landon wiped at his mouth.

I didn't answer, turning on my heel to walk down the hallway. I wanted yell at him, but it seemed as though that wasn't an option. So instead, I sought to find the bathroom, to wash off my hands, and neck. Not looking at him made me calm down a bit. It made me think clearly without wanting to jump at him right in the middle of the hallway.

"Where are you going?" He asked, surprised at my sudden departure. I didn't know really. Alden hadn't shown us where the bathrooms were, so I was hoping for the best. Landon trailed behind me. This blood, that was slowly drying, needed to go instantly.

"I need to wash off the blood," I snap. Landon sighed deeply.

"The bathroom is back this way," he informs me. I stop in my tracks, roll my eyes, and walk back the way I had come. I narrow my eyes at a smirking Landon as I pass him, bumping my shoulder against his. Even touching him made me jump. The obvious tingles were exchanged like germs; frequently, and in large doses.

"Listen Al, trust me when I say it was going to happen eventually. And I didn't want to wait," Landon stated from behind me. My heart skipped a beat at his words. I had dreamed of him telling me these things, but *after* he had marked me with my permission. This was hardly romantic...

"But here? We aren't even within our own packs walls," I reply over my shoulder. Landon still walked securely behind me. It would be so embarrassing to walk back into the dining room, suddenly mated to the Alpha of the Power Pack. I took a deep breath. That was a lot to process at this one time.

Eventually I found a bathroom. It was small, but a basin, mirror and running water was all that was needed at the moment. I entered the bathroom, with Landon following suit. I quickly turned the tap, and watched the water flow out of the facet.

I looked at Landon behind me first, who was watching my eyes, before I looked at myself.

Apart from the blood staining the left side of my neck, I looked rejuvenated in a way. My eyes were bright and alert, and weren't dark underneath from the lack of sleep I seemed to be getting lately. My skin was smooth and flawless almost, with no imperfections to be seen. Slowly, I brought my hand up to my face to see if I was real.

"Do I really look like this?" I question, noticing that even my posture was improved. Landon nodded from behind me.

"Marking you has enhanced your well-being. Your lack of a mate beforehand was depleting your overall health," Landon explained. I never knew that. Some things I wish they taught me before I left school. Of course he would know...

"And the fact that you're now mated to an Alpha helps too," he added. I swallowed. I was mated to an Alpha now...An Alpha of a Pack that holds a lot of responsibility over other Packs. I was a Luna, a leader. Shit...

Shaking these things in my head away, I concentrate on washing the blood of my neck. I didn't realise it would initially hurt this much, and create a bucket load of blood. I shiver, watching it all wash down the drain.

Once all the blood was gone, I assessed the side of my neck. Two marks, slightly swollen tainted my neck. It was a mark that was bound to scare any male from my near vicinity. Slowly I begin to shift my hair over the mark, covering it completely. Landon frowns at my movement.

"Why are you covering it?" Landon asks, moving to stand beside me. I sigh deeply, and turn to him, looking him in the eye. He looked hurt, and I didn't mean to offend him, it was just the fact that we were here, with company.

"It's not going to look very good if we walk back into that room, suddenly mated," I reason. He shrugged, obviously not fazed by that at all. He probably didn't mind showing Cyrus that I was no longer an unmated female.

"Alden will smell it anyway, and who cares what Cyrus thinks," Landon dismisses. I close my eyes, feeling a headache beginning to form. I couldn't do that to Cyrus. Landon might think it's the best thing in the world, but my heart couldn't take it. Annoyed, I push at his chest.

"Where are you going?" He questioned. I gave him a deadpan look, giving him another push. He smirks at me, obviously entertained by my actions. Slowly he pulled my hair away from my neck, where it was covering the mark.

"Back to the dining room, where everyone is waiting for us," I reply. I want to push him again, but touching him makes me weaken. So instead, I try to duck under his arms to get out the door. Landon was quick to grab me by my arms, and put me back where I was; trapped against the basin.

"Landon, can you move please?" I ask sweetly. He tilts his head, giving me a smile. I knew he wasn't going to move out of my way without persuasion.

"I don't know, can I?" He asks coyly. I sigh, narrowing my eyes at him. He answers my glare with a chuckle. I never knew Landon to be like this. He was always so reserved around me. I had seen his stubborn side in many things, but never sexually.

"Yes, you are perfectly capable of moving out of my way," I say simply. His arms rest against the basin behind me still, his face centimetres from mine. I stare straight into his eyes, showing him he can't push me around.

Suddenly he leans in, his lips enchantingly close to my ear.

"Make me," he whispers, causing me to shiver. He removes one arm from trapping me in, using his hand instead run up my side.

Giving in, I grab his face between my hands, and guide his lips to mine. He responds immediately, thrusting his tongue urgently into my mouth. His dominance was obvious, as he grips my hips strongly, lifting me up to sit on the basin.

I run my fingers through my hair, feeling his need through our kiss. Less than an hour ago, I could never have imagined I would be mated to this man. Touching him was so *different* now. It was as though he gave me an unexplainable strength it every little touch and kiss.

"Landon," I breath, as he pulls away, kissing down my neck. Memories from only minutes before flood back. His teeth sinking into my neck, as he claimed me as his own. It makes my eyes open, from being blissfully closed. But as soon as his soft lips touch the mark, that still stung slightly, I sunk back into his arms.

"Well then."

I jump, hearing a deep, rather scarred voice. Landon whirls around, obviously knowing exactly who was there without even seeing him. I gazed over his shoulder, seeing Alden standing at the door, looking shocked, his eyebrows raised to his hairline.

Fear courses through me, but apart from being slightly shocked, it didn't seem as though Alden was all that fazed.

"I must say, I saw it coming... you two mating. But I can't say I predicted it happening in the bathroom of my home," Alden says softly. I want to correct him, to say it *didn't* actually happen in the bathroom, but I refrain.

I don't know what summoned the Alpha in the first place, but it can't have been too important as he turns around, and goes back the way he came. I let out a deep breath of relief. Landon helps me off the basin, so my feet hit the ground easily. I was slightly wary of his attentive attitude, but I don't question it.

"Shall we get back to lunch, my girl?" He asks warmly.

My girl.

Chapter Thirteen

Walking back into that dining room was one of the worst things I have ever done. Not because everyone knew immediately that I was now a marked female, but because Cyrus looked so happy to see me, even though I had walked in with Landon and Alden.

"Shall we continue?" Alden asks, as we took our seats again. Natasha leant over and whispered in Landon's ear. Obviously, I didn't catch what she had said, but Landon didn't seem too happy about it. He shook his head, frowning deeply. Melia just sat there, as Alden once again slung his arm over Melia's shoulder.

It seemed as though Cyrus and Melia were getting along quite well, which was unnerving Alpha Alden. I, on the other hand was too busy dealing with my own problems. All I could feel was the mark on my neck, stinging and burning slightly. Luckily, I was seated right next to Landon, so it wasn't bothering me too much.

"Althea, I was talking to Alden while you were gone. He said that there would be plenty of room here in this Pack for *us*," Cyrus said suddenly, making the whole table go quiet. This conversation obviously was exchanged before Alden found out I was mated to Landon.

I felt Landon stiffen next to me, not at all pleased by what Cyrus was insinuating.

"You want me to move here?" I question. I didn't really want to ask this, because we weren't even mated. Moving in together was something that wasn't even addressed till a pair was mated. Cyrus shrugged carelessly.

"Eventually. I think this is a great place to start a-"

"A what, sorry?" Landon cut in. I glanced warily at him, to see he was gritting his teeth, his jaw clenching beyond belief. I could see in his eyes that he was beyond livid, even though expression remained moderately impassive, which was much more intimidating.

"What's not to love about the Power Pack?" I question, cutting in before Cyrus can say something stupid, that would surely ruin everything. The stare off between Landon and Cyrus was frightening, but I seemed to be the only one noticing it fully. Natasha was too busy checking out Alden. Alden was too busy checking out Melia. Melia was too busy not caring...

"There isn't anything wrong with it. I was just thinking, that maybe branching out would be better for the both of us," Cyrus explained. Even as he said that, he wasn't looking at me, but Landon. I rolled my eyes, knowing neither of the Wolves were paying any attention to me.

"Althea isn't leaving the Pack," Landon said deeply, his voice so intimidating, it sent a shiver up my spine. Cyrus narrowed his eyes, like he was expecting the challenge that Landon was issuing.

"What makes you think that?" Cyrus questions. I sigh.

"I am the Alpha, and I'm mated to Al-"

"So how long is this lunch supposed to go on for, because I am expected somewhere for dinner, and we need to get back in time," Natasha says, cutting Landon off completely. I let out a sigh of relief, glad for her random intervention that truly saved me.

"We should leave now. Thank you, Alden, for your hospitality," Landon said, pushing his chair back so he could stand. We all followed suit.

Our departure was quick. The tension between us all was obvious. After thanking Alden, and saying goodbye to Melia, we piled into the car again, and set off.

I was glad to be away from that Pack, hoping silently that Landon and Cyrus wouldn't talk to each other for the rest of the ride back home. That wish wasn't completely in vain, considering they weren't the real problem.

I was stuck in the backseat with Landon again, who was trying to make conversation with me. I wanted to talk to him, but every time I opened my mouth, I saw Cyrus's eyes flicker up to he mirror, so he could see into the backseat. So instead, I sat with my arms crossed, staring out the window at the endless countryside.

"Do you not have *any* music in this metal death-trap?" Natasha asked Cyrus from the front seat. I looked up, wishing I could see the whole of Cyrus's face. All I could see was Cyrus's eyebrows crease together in the rear-view mirror.

"Maybe in the glove box," he mumbled. I watched as Natasha blandly shuffled through disks in the compartment. I didn't understand what her problem was, considering the fact that we had driven all the way there without any issues. She plucks one out, looking over it with interest.

"Can you speed up a bit, you're going to slow," Natasha orders, taking the disk from its cover. I lean forward, looking between the two seats.

"Shut up would you," I snap. I wanted to say that I didn't intend to say that, but really, I did. Natasha feel deathly silent, before turning in my seat to look me dead in the eye.

There is something unnerving frightening about coming eye to eye with a *snake*, who you know is probably going to kill you, but you aren't too scared to it. Instead, all you want to do is punch it square in the jaw.

"Excuse me?" She spluttered. She looked as though I had just insulted her great ancestors, or had just stolen from her family's private bank account. Nobody else in the car dare spoke, as I death stared the girl in the front seat.

"You heard me; shut up. Nobody wants to hear you complain," I exclaim I'm disgust. Natasha sits back in her seat, after staring me down for an unpleasant amount of time. Wordlessly, she tosses the CD back onto the ground.

It was obvious that the little Queen wasn't used to being talked to like that, and I took great pleasure I'm dishing it to her on a silver platter...

"You're only saying things to impress Landon," she whispered under her breath. I only *just* caught what she had mumbled, but it was enough to send me hurling over the seat. Soon enough I had her silky hair fisted in my hand.

"Woah," Landon said in surprise from behind me, grabbing my arms. Cyrus swerved ridiculously across the road, acting in shock from my sudden attack on Natasha. Landon attempted to pry Natasha's hair from my tight grip, but I wasn't having it, trying to elbow him away from me.

"Get off me bitch," Natasha snapped, trying to fight me off. Cyrus pulled to the side of the road, the back wheels skidding on gravel. A car honked their horn in protest from behind us, before speeding past. Landon had managed to get one hand off Natasha, intertwining his fingers with one.

"Al, calm down," Landon coaxed firmly, but his voice was baby soft. I couldn't believe this...He was calming me down already, which I didn't want at all. Meanwhile, Cyrus had come to a complete stop at the side of the road.

In a hurry, I ripped my hands from her hair, enjoying her hiss of pain. I cracked the door open, and stepped outside onto the road, before rounding the car. Cyrus watched me with disbelief, obviously surprised considering he had never seen me like this before.

Fiercely, Natasha stepped out, coming to face me square on. Her make-up was smudged across her face, and her hair was ruffled slightly. I wasn't scared of her at all.

"Is this what you want? To fight me for Landon? Because bitch I wil-"

I cut her off by punching her square in the jaw.

60

She stumbled back, clutching her face in surprise. I was even slightly surprised that I even had the strength in me for to throw such a punch. I watched as Landon brushed past me, moving over to see if Natasha was badly hurt.

"Get off me," she hissed, brushing Landon away. She looked at me again her eyes blazing with the exact same anger that was streaming through my veins. She takes a shuddering step forward, and I glance over her shoulder at the ditch behind her, filled with dirty water.

With an idea in my head, I step forward till there was hardly any space between us. I was about to push on her shoulders, and send her toppling into the water, but I felt hands on my waist, pulling me away from the current situation.

"It's okay," I say, dismissing Cyrus, how had a strong hold on my waist, as he tried to keep me from attacking Natasha again. I turned in his grip and looked at him. He looked terrified; probably of me.

"Are you okay now?" He asked in my ear. I nod, pulling away slightly. Landon was making sure Natasha wasn't damaged, although we all knew she was already sufficiently messed up mentally.

I could feel his disapproval, when he saw Cyrus's proximity to me.

"We should go now, and if you two fight again, you are both dead," Landon growled.

Chapter Fourteen

I was back here again, my mate lounging beside me. It was the same field we usually met in most mornings, back when we were only friends.

It was early morning, and we had decided to meet up to discuss what had happened at that dinner not less than a day ago. My hair blew softly behind me in the gentle breeze, the grass touching my legs lightly. Everything was so calm, on comparison to what was going on in my mind.

"So, when are you moving your belongings to my place?" Landon suddenly asked, his voice intruding the warm place in my mind where I was thinking. I flinched, turning to look him in the eye.

He looked beyond handsome, with his soft skin glowing in the morning sun, his green eyes illuminating his feelings, and his slightly too long hair was pushed back by the breeze. He was mine now...

"You realise that I have to tell Cyrus before anything can happen," I proclaim, my finger twirling around a stem of grass, only to yank it from the ground. Landon made a rather disgusted face as I uttered Cyrus's name. He still hated that guy, and I knew if I told him about the perfume, he might kill him or something.

"When will you do that?" He questions bluntly. I shrug, looking off into the distance, trying to sort my thoughts out.

"Today, I promise," I say, coming to a final decision. I didn't want to keep this going any longer. Having to lie to him only makes the situation first. My plan was to show him the mark upon my neck, and be done with it.

Landon nodded.

"And your parents?" He adds. I had thought about telling numerous times, but I know my father is going to be less than approving. I have resisted telling them by covering the mark as best as my abilities allow. That basically included always wearing my hair down, wearing a high neck line, and I even tried wearing some of my mother's make-up.

"Soon enough, although I'm not looking forward to telling them," I admit, running a piece of grass up and down the side of my leg in disinterest. Landon chuckles, knowing my pain.

"You could just move in with me," Landon suggest casually. I blink. Move in with him? It *had* crossed my mind before, but hearing it come from his mouth made it so much more real. The fact that the man I had crushed on for a major portion of my life was now my mate, and wanted to live with me seemed unreal.

"And your father?"

"He will come around eventually," he excuses. We both sit in silence, thinking about things for a moment. Suddenly, Landon glanced at his watch, checking the time.

"I better go, I have a meeting with the Alpha's this afternoon. Will you be okay with Cyrus?" He asks. I nod, giving him a weak smile.

The worst that could happen was Cyrus lashes out at me in anger, which I highly doubt would happen, considering Cyrus had pretty mellow personality. In saying that, he *had* seemed to be a little overbearing when it came to Landon.

"I'll be fine, call me as often as you can," I say firmly. Don't blame me, I was just making sure my mate wasn't going to get into any trouble while I was gone. For all I know, most of the Alpha's are unmated, so I would hate to know how many unmated females hanging around.

Landon smiled softly, leaning closer to brush a piece of stray hair from my face. I gazed at him, wondering how someone so attractive could be into me.

"Someone jealous?" He questioned, smirking. I gently pushed on his chest, rolling my eyes. He wishes...Although he is right. I didn't think I was the kind of person to be territorial over something like a man.

"Hardly. What could I possibly be jealous of?" I inquired. Landon seemed to think for a moment, before rolling over, pinning my body against the soft *down like* grass. I stare up at him curiously, as he lifts my left leg up, so it rests near his hip.

"So you wouldn't mind if I talked to other girls then?" He chuckled at me, his breathing brushing against my lips. I narrowed my eyes at him, as if to warn him.

"I never said you couldn't *talk* to girls, just don't touch them, that's all," I clarify knowingly. Landon nodded, still lightly laughing at what I had to say. I was being serious too, so he better take that into consideration...

"Don't worry Al, you're the only one for me," he stated firmly. I smiled, as he finally leaned in, pressing his soft lips against mine. There was no place I would rather be, than with my mate.

Slowly, I ran the tips of my fingers down Landon back, feeling every muscle pulse and move. I cupped his face gently, his tender skin feeling amazing against my hands, as he moved his lips against mine.

All too soon, he pulled away.

"I should go huh?" He muttered, pulling away from me, so he could stand up. I just lay in the long grass, watching him. Wordlessly, he pulled his shirt off like it was the natural thing to do. I frowned at him, but secretly I was enjoying the view.

"I need to shift, and I'm not so keen about destroying my clothes," he explained with a chuckle, noticing the strange look I was giving him. He dumped his dark blue shirt onto the ground beside me.

He looked so beautiful, standing above me. The awakening sun illuminated his skin, detailing his chiselled torso, while making his skin look golden and soft. I was then taken by surprise, as he casually dropped his slacks.

"Landon, what the hell?" I shrieked, covering my eyes from the sight that nearly stole my innocent. I heard him laughing animatedly, as I shielded myself in darkness. I was *not* going to deal with this right now.

"What's wrong sweetheart?" He asked coyly. Internally I rolled my eyes.

"What if someone sees you here...Naked?" I question. It was as though Landon didn't care about his reputation as an Alpha at all. It was especially important that he watches himself now that we are mated.

"Don't act like it's not natural to shift," he exclaimed cynically. Maybe a good ten years ago, when Wolves shifted literally every moment of their lives. These days, it's slightly less socially acceptable to waltz around naked. Maybe Landon didn't know because he hadn't been exposed to the realities of life.

"You're going to see me naked eventually Althea," he added cheekily.

"It was nice seeing you Landon. You better go before you're late," I farewell, waving my free hand blindly in the air. I felt him lay a gentle kiss on my forehead, before I rush of air hit me. I nervously uncover my hand, to see his running across the field at a remarkable pace, the hair if his dark Wolf glinting in the sunlight.

I sigh and stand up. Time to confront Cyrus

"You want to tell me what's wrong?" Cyrus asks. Looking at his face right now; so concerned, broke my heart. I didn't want to let him down like this, but I couldn't keep this from him.

We sat on my couch at home. I had told Cyrus that what I needed to say was urgent. It was *really*. I just hoped that he took the news well, rather than her mad at me for something could hardly control.

"Please don't be mad," I say softly. Cyrus nods, then something in his deep blue eyes click, like he's remembered something amazing.

"Wait first! I have something amazing to tell you," he rushed. It was as though his whole being seemed to lit up. I motioned for him to continue. I didn't want to kill his mood just yet. He paused briefly, like he was creating an effect between us.

"Alden called, saying he would love to have us in his Pack!"

I blinked.

Alden, the little-

"So that means we will be able to move there, as soon as possible," he proclaimed in utter excitement. In my whole time of knowing him, I had never seen him look so genuinely excited about something.

"Together?" I squeaked. He didn't realise what impeccable timing he had. He nodded eagerly.

"Isn't it great?"

I sighed, and grabbed his hand. I could tell he was slightly confused about my grim expression.

"I need to tell you something," I say softly. He sits up a little, fully interested in what I had to say. His fingers played with my own gently.

"I'm now mate-"

A brisk knock on the door cut me off, as well as giving me a massive fright. Cyrus looked at me, his eyebrows creased in wonder. Who could that be, at this time? Not my parents, that's for sure.

I stood up, and wandered over to the door. I took another glance at Cyrus before swinging the door open. And there stood two uniformed guards, handcuffs dangling from their fingers.

"We are here to arrest you on suspicion of the disappearance of Natasha Javilor," the man states bluntly. My eyes widen.

What?

Chapter Fifteen

I had never been so angry in my life.

There was no way, *no* damn way I had anything to do with the disappearance of Landon's stupid date he brought to the Wisdom Pack with us. Unless of course our argument scared her off to another Pack. That I could only wish for.

I sat in the back of a prison kind of car. I had been shoved in the back of it, with the woman guard alongside me. I was binded with handcuffs, which were digging into my tender wrists. They were treating me like a real criminal...just wait till Landon hears about this.

Cyrus had protested with me, obviously not keen on me getting taken away to some destination that even I wasn't aware of. The guards were being very faint within their responses, which only made me more livid. I could only imagine how shocked Cyrus had been, before I even got to tell him the news, watching me get dragged away like a fugitive.

We were driving toward Landon's home, and already I'm anxious. What happens if his father's there? There is no Landon to protect and defend me from his wrath.

By the time we got there, I swear I probably had rusted away at the handcuffs due to my profuse amount of sweating. I was pulled from the car, as harshly as I had been pushed in, and stood in front of the bonnet of the car. It was then, a bag was shoved roughly over my head, and all went black.

***

By the time I woke up, all prior knowledge on the time and day had flown out of my head completely. I didn't know where I was, all I knew was that it was dark, and I was lying on cool, hard ground.

The smell was so gravely familiar. It provoked nausea in my stomach. The putrid smell of dirty bodies and old food was practically suffocating, I

67

wasn't sure if I was going to make it out of here alive. But I knew where I was, as soon as *he* spoke.

"Guess who's back?"

Him... Kace. The man who had been locked down here beforehand. The total creep who I had to share space with, back when I tried to break into Landon's home. Although technically, it wasn't breaking in that I was doing, but simply visiting.

I could only imagine how much entertainment this brought him.

"You're the real criminal here, not me," he stated joyfully. Weakly, I pulled myself off the floor, so I was partially sitting up. That smell was really getting to me, and so was my lack of vision. And the yearning for Landon was burning my insides. I gritted my teeth; there was no time to act pathetic.

"Shut it, we need to find a way out," I snap, trying to get my feet to stay stable under my body. Kace sounded like he was pushed against the back wall, while I stayed closer to the front of the cage, where the air was slightly clearer. My hands grabbed the dense metal that stopped me from reaching freedom.

"I've been locked in this prison for years sweetheart, I don't think *you* will be able to find a way out. No offence," Kace replies cynically. I narrowed my eyes, pushing my weight against the bars. His comments only tainted my determination, rather than diminishing it completely.

"That's because you obviously didn't attempt every option," I panted, finding this more difficult then I had first thought. Okay, maybe I wasn't strong enough for this; I needed to use my brains.

"I've been here seven years, trust me, I've tried," he stated firmly. He sounded frustrated, but it didn't stop me. Using my brain to figure this out was my only option. I was starting to realise my urgency, as my eyes were starting to adjust to the harsh light. Could Landon not feel the bond between us? Did he not realise I was distressed, or were we too far away, I mean, he *is* in a completely different Pack.

"I'm not rotting in this place," I asserted. I heard Kace sigh, probably getting sick of my complaining. I rested my forehead against the bars, wanting to cry, to scream...to her Landon back. Where was he when I most desperately need him?

"Why you in here again? Thought you were *close* with the Alpha," Kace commented. I close my eyes, letting my body fall into a sitting position in the floor. Why was I here? This was injustice, I hadn't hurt anybody, and I surely wasn't the reason that Natasha had gone missing.

"I was framed for something I didn't do. Some stupid girl ran away and now it's *my* fault," I vent, my back against the bars. I silently hoped no one would come up behind me.

"Sounds familiar," Kace muttered. I frown. "It does?"

I could imagine him nodding in response, as I couldn't see him through the thick darkness.

"My brother... He tends to get in trouble a lot, and I'm always the one who gets in trouble for it. Your stupid friend Landon locked me up here for absolutely no reason," he told me, his voice soft and breathless. It pained me to hear him say that, but I didn't know the full story enough to judge him, or accept his innocence.

"He's not just my friend," I say softly. I listen to Kace shift, maybe getting closer. "Carry on..."

"He's my... My mate," I say quickly. I don't know where the audacity to tell him came from, but I felt like I needed to share it with someone. He coughed nervously, probably not expecting it.

"Seriously?" He spluttered. A suddenly surge of growls filled the room from behind me, inmates within the cells hearing the news. I back away from the bars, and over to where I assumed Kace was. I didn't want to be too close to him, but the unstable prison dwellers scared me more than anything.

"Yeah, it's not like I asked for it," I whisper. The growls were so threatening, so brutally *real*, like nothing I had heard before. But I wasn't about to admit that to Kace. He would probably laugh in my face.

"He marked you without your permission? You know there is a way to be unmat-"

"Don't even insinuate that," I interjected, before he could even say it. I knew there was some sort of voodoo way to be unmated, but I wasn't having it. Landon had made the choice to mark me, and it was something that I had dreamed about previously.

"You're sure you like him?" He questions. He suddenly sounds a lot closer. Uncomfortable close, but I'm already pressed ridiculously up to the corner of the cell. What if he rapes me or something? I have no Landon here to help me out of the situation. I have to get myself out.

A sudden brilliant, yet slightly stupid idea popped into my head. I scrambled to my feet. This could work, I could make it out of here if I execute this right!

I walk to the bars, and begin shaking them furiously. This gets the attention of the rest of the inmates, who's eyes I can feel on me.

"Hey Guard, come look at what I can do," I call out loudly, following this with another shake of the bars. They rattled loudly, and I knew the Guard patrolling the end of the hallway would hear.

"What are you doing?" Kace questioned nervously. How had none of these psychopathic prison goers thought if this before. Through the darkness, I just managed to see one of the Guards running toward me. I had to do this, before I thought twice about it.

Landon wasn't here to save me, so I guess I have to do this myself.

The Guard skidded to a stop in front of the cell, and I could make out the slick surface of his baton. He was ready if I tried to escape. I didn't want to know how many times Kace probably received beatings from the Guards here. Not saying he didn't deserve it, because he probably did.

"What is it? You're stirring up the others," he spat gruffly. I couldn't see his face, which made this a whole lot easier. Bracing my feet on the ground, I slid my hands through the bars, reaching out toward him.

And before he could even register what I was doing, I grabbed his shoulders between my small hands, and violently thrust him toward me. The sound of bone against metal rung out loudly, as the Guard's head smacked fully against the bar. I hadn't meant for him to be *that* easy to pull, but my plan seemed to work.

They stopped moving, stilling completely in my hands. He slumped forward, as I removed my hands, falling in a heap of the ground. Did I seriously just do that?

"What did you do?" Kace screeched. I heard the rustle of clothes as he stood up. I don't know what I did, but whatever it was, was nothing like what I had ever attempted in my life. Everyone else in the close vicinity was shocked into silence, except Kace, who had come to stand beside me.

"Holy shit, that was badass!" he emphasised in disbelief. The Guard was knocked out cold, the batton having rolled away somewhere from his grasp. No one had said I was *badass* before, not that I knew what it meant, I presumed it was a good thing...

"We need to get the key off his body," I implore hurriedly. I was afraid more Guards were going to emerge from the darkness and beat me to death. Even through the darkness, I could see the outline of Kace's head as he nodded. Everything was starting to seem a lot clearer now.

I could even see Kace knell down, and reach his hand through the bar to get to the Guard's body. *Luckily, he had fallen close enough*, I thought as Kace patted along his waist line, looking for his keys. The sudden jingle of keys flooded my body with some type of warmth.

It was strange, I had been in this cell for mere hours, and freedom seemed a distance memory. I wanted to escape *so* badly, I could only imagine how Kace felt.

He pulled back, golden keys dangling on his fingers. He turned to me, resting his hands on my shoulders. It was then that I could see the cool blue eyes through the darkness.

"You saved us!"

He removes his hands, and turns to the door again. I watch nervously as he unlocked the door, bending his arm backwards to get the key in the hole.

Suddenly it flings open, and we burst out. The cells erupt in brutal screams, as prisons called at us for release, pressing their faces up against the bars like animals in a circus show. It was horrifying.

"We have to let them out," I say loudly, pulling Kace back. He had attempted to run toward the door, but I had stopped him.

"They are hardly Wolves, they don't deserve Freedom," he snapped, pulling at my shirt. Taken one last glance into the shadows, I let him drag me toward Freedom.

Chapter Sixteen

Seeing the light of day was something I have never cherished so much till this moment. Sure, it had blinded me at first, making me stumble around incoherently, swiping out for Kace. He was still squinting after a good ten minutes of being outside.

"Things haven't changed, I see," he mused, gazing around, his eyes still half shut. We had managed to make it as far as Landon's back yard. It wouldn't take long for the Guards to discover they had escaped, and come after us. Now what, I'm going to be a fugitive for the rest of my life?

No, I had to call Landon and get him back to the Pack as soon as possible.

"You can see," I questioned widely. My vision was back in full swing, but it seemed as though Kace was still having a hard time. I watched him stumble over a small hole in the ground, and land on the grass. Even in this tense situation, I could find ridicule in the man in front of me.

If you could even call him that.

Kace was hardly what I expected. I'm fact, the shock of dirty blond hair upon his head didn't suit him at all. His eyes were a washed out blue, like they had been lacking sunlight, which quite frankly they *had* been. His whole being lacked vitamin D. He was pale, lethargic looking, and most definitely needed a bath.

He lay sprawled on the grass, face pushed into the dirt. Someone was enjoying this a little *too* much.

"Come on, we got to get out of here before we get caught," I say, kicking the back of his leg. I feel like I probably should be scared of Kace. He was in prison originally, and Landon didn't seem so keen on him when I mentioned him. But out here, in the open world, Kace was different.

For a start, Kace hasn't been out here since he was twelve. He's fairly unfit, but undernourished. He couldn't hurt me, not when I could run faster than his lanky legs could carry him. He had an unexplainable scar down the side of the neck, and I would hate to ask what it was.

Kace heaved himself up off the ground carelessly, looking over his shoulder at me. I had to admit, his eyes were strangely captivating. Not in the attractive way, but in a way that had me curious. I wanted to know how he got them like that, but that was probably a stupid question.

I knew we had to take the back way. Scale the concrete wall that guarded the interior. Beyond it was the field Landon usually cut through to get to me every morning. Once we made it there, we would be safe.

"We need to get over that wall," I state blandly, glancing at mountain of concrete. Kace made a face at it, not too happy about our predicament.

"There is *no* way," he pointed out cynically. He was right, the wall was there to stop people like Kace and I. We *had* to put the front way.

I lean over and grab Kace's arm, yanking him with me. The front of the house was probably guarded, but maybe we could sneak out. Peering around the side of the house, I was surprised at what I saw. No guards...No, nothing.

I blinked. Was this a trap?

"What are you waiting for?" Kace questioned, moving past me, toward the gate. I frowned at him, but he kept walking, like nothing in the world could possible hold him back. He sauntered across the courtyard, a spring in his step.

I followed behind warily, looking both ways for any sign of Guards. Kace didn't seem to mind at all, as he approached a black miss on the ground. I jogged closer, wondering what it was.

It was a person; a Guard. They were lying against the gate - the open gate. Why an unconscious Guard was there, gun laying dangerously beside him? Kace waltzed up to him, without a care in the world, picked up the gun, and turned it over in his hands.

"Are you crazy? Put that *thing,* away," I shrieked, pausing before I got any closer. Kace paused, glancing over at me. He looked dangerous, the gun poised in his hand, probably fully loaded with the safety off. He could shoot and kill me at any moment he pleased, and still cleanly make a break for it.

How could I have been so stupid as to trust him? Trust him with something like my freedom? Landon was right, Kace was in that prison for a reason. These were my thoughts, until he did something unexpected...

He dropped the gun back into the ground, and shrugged.

"You're right, let's go," he hurried, turning his back to me. I blinked, before quickly following behind him. Okay, maybe I was quick to judge him, but the man was handling a gun only moments ago!

We quickly walked beside each other, till Kace said he would hang back to make sure no Guards were coming. We were barely out of the gates, before all hell broke loose.

Two Guards suddenly jumped out of nowhere. They grabbed my arms from both sides. They must have been camping out, waiting for Kace and I to step one foot from Landon's home territory. That was the first that came to my mind anyway.

"Get on the ground," one of them yelled rudely in my ear. I winced, as I was forced to my knees, pressing them against the gravel ground. One of them attempted to shove a piece of cloth in my mouth, until two shots rang out around them.

The Guards fall unconscious, or rather, *dead* beside me.

"Well, wasn't exactly expecting that now were we..." Kace mused, walking past me. I looked up, my mouth open, two dead Wolves beside me, at the man in front of me. He dropped the gun; the same gun that had ended these seemingly innocent lives.

Kace turned and held his hand out of me. I stared at it, like it was about to wrap around my neck and end my life. He stared at me expectantly with his curious blue eyes. Panic had ceased my heart, making it beat irregularly, so it felt as though I was about to pass out.

"You killed them?" I spluttered, gaping at him. I didn't even want to turn and look at the Guards, that were beside me. Kace did though, eyeing the bodies with interest.

"Well yeah."

"Why?"

"They were going to catch you again, and you don't want know what would have happened to you if I let them," Kace said seriously. So seriously, it took me by surprise. "Why do *you* think they went for you, and not me?"

I hadn't thought about that.

"Look, you can come with me, or you can stay here while they get more Guards," he stated. He turned, and began walking away. He almost looked funny, wearing only a pair of ripped pants and a loose shirt. He wasn't even wearing shoes.

I stood up, making sure I didn't touch the bodies. If I had, I would have thrown up.

Eventually, after quite some walking, silently might I add, Kace stopped. We were minutes from my house, not that I would have let Kace come there with me. But I didn't expect for him to know exactly where he was going.

"No offence, but I think we need to split off," he said, making me stop also. I turn back to him, seeing him look at me meekly.

"No, you're right. Do you know where you're going-"

"Yes," he cut in curtly. It was then that he turned around, without another word and walked away. I stared at his departing walk, and slight hobble. He didn't turn back, and I couldn't help wonder where he was going. It seemed as though he was late for something, but the only thing I could think of, was him being late for the last seven years of his life.

I didn't call after him, it was worth it. Instead I turned and walked back toward my home. No doubt my parents would be worried, and so would Cyrus. But I am only in the mood for one person, and that's my mate.

Unsurprisingly, my parents weren't home. The house was locked up, so I had to sneak in the door without a closed lock, that nobody knew about. Once I was inside, I headed straight toward the phone.

At first, Landon didn't pick up when I called. I hope he wasn't in the middle of a meeting, but then again, the time difference from where he is suggests it would be some time at night. On the third call, I assumed he was asleep, and was about to give up when I heard a husky voice on the other end of the line.

"Landon, it's Althea," I say quickly into the phone. I'm sitting cross-legged on my couch, wondering what to say. How does 'I escaped prison, and your father probably want to kill me' sound?

"Hey Al, how are you?" He asks. It's a loose question, a question he expects an easy answer to, like good. But quite frankly, I was hardly *good*.

"I'm in trouble," I say. I find myself glancing over my shoulder, scared a Guard is going to jump out at me. And drag me back to that filthy prison again.

"How?"

"I don't know. I escaped prison-"

"What, why were you in prison?" He questioned. I breathe in slowly.

"I'm not exactly sure. Apparently, Natasha has gone missing... they blamed it on me," I exclaim. Landon goes quiet, as he takes in the news. I knew that *he* knew his father had something to do with it.

"I'll be home as soon as I can. We will figure it out then," he said so quickly I almost didn't catch it. I frowned.

"Landon, you have your meeting, I just need you to-"

"No. I'm coming home Althea, I'm not leaving you again." And that was that, he hung up. I sighed in frustration, throwing my phone back on the couch carelessly. He wouldn't be back for a while; it took many hours to travel back, no matter what transport he used.

I stand, glancing over at the clock mounted in the wall. It was still early, but I wanted to sleep to pass time. And anyway, my head was aching, and I needed to lay low, in case Guards were out. It wouldn't be long till they found me, if they do, and I knew sleep would be perfect to take my mind of it.

So, I trundle to my bedroom, Landon in mind. *I hope he gets here soon.*

Chapter Seventeen

When I woke, it was the next day. I was only woken by the stream of light coming through the window. Damn, I definitely should have closed my curtains last night, before I fell into bed, with my clothes from yesterday still on.

I rolled out of bed, my toes touching the familiar, soft carpet of my bedroom. I was home, *safe*, and Landon should be back to the Pack soon, if not now. Checking the time, it was only seven in the morning.

I still feel drowsy and slightly sick, so I decide a shower would be the best cure. After checking out the window to make sure I hadn't woken to Guards holding me hostage from outside my house. Everything was clear, beside my suspicion.

Grabbing some fresh clothes, and a towel, I crack open my bedroom door. I can hear my parents bustling around downstairs. The kettle was boiling, newspaper was being ruffled. Everything was how I should be on a normal morning for them. It didn't seem as though they were missing me too much.

I had the sudden urge to walk down those stairs and let my parents deal with this. But I knew that they would be more of a hindrance, then a help to the situation. The Alpha, *Landon,* would be the only one who could get me out of being killed. By his own father...

Once I had closed myself in the bathroom safely, I let out a breath. Hopefully my parents wouldn't hear the sound of the shower running, since the hot water pipes tend to rattle.

Placing a clean towel on the hook, I switched in the shower, and stripped of my clothes. It felt nice to shower, after being stuck in that prison. I also gave me the opportunity to think; about Landon, Cyrus, my parents. Even Kace lingered in the back of my mind.

Once I was closed inside the bathroom, I let out a deep breath I had been holding.

I showered quickly, sure to not waste any time. I did not have any plans so far, but getting to Landon was one of them.

I dressed promptly, towel dried my hair, and walked out of the bathroom. I was about to walk back to my bedroom, when a familiar voice caught my attention.

"I am sorry I didn't come early Miss. I was just in a state of shock, that's all."

"Oh Cyrus, come in and tell me what you mean."

I cringe, so deeply, I probably gave myself permanent frown lines. Cyrus had come here, still thinking he was to be my mate, about to ruin everything.

I stumble toward the tip of the stairs, and peer down. From here I see nothing but the dining table, my parents' uneaten breakfast strews about. I jump, as I see mother appear in view, making me cower more into the shadows. She quickly clears the dishes away, and disappears from view.

Cyrus is then in view, sitting down at the head of the table, looking solemn. He crosses his hands together, and rests them I'm the table. He didn't look as distraught as I would have been if he had been dragged to prison for a crime he did not commit. He looked fresh, well dressed like he was ready to impress.

And it wasn't as though he hadn't impressed my parents enough already...

"Cyrus," I say in a rushed whisper. He looks up, frowning. When he glances at me, he looks beyond surprised. He goes to say something, but I shake my head vigorously, holding my finger to my lips. Now he looks beyond confused.

I motion for him to come up the stair, but before I can do anything, my parents are at the table.

"Excuse me, can I use your bathroom?" Cyrus asks politely, though sounding nervous. I can already feel the onslaught of questions coming, that I probably don't have any answer to.

They tell him where the bathroom is, and he quickly jogs up the stairs. I decide to drag him to my room, where I know we can talk without my parents interrupting.

"Care to explain?"

"You can't tell my parents I was taken to prison, they will freak out," I say. It's true, I would hate to see their reaction. Cyrus runs his hands through his thick black hair, looking frustrated.

"So, they did take you to prison?"

"Technically yes, but it was all a misunderstanding. They let me go in the end," I say. Let me go, more like I escaped and so did another detainee. He *had* told me he wasn't guilty of anything, but that stunt he pulled, shooting those Guards, made me begin to question why I had actually helped him out with me.

"So, you're free now?" He questioned. I nod. I was back home, safe. I repeated it was a misunderstanding. I should be considered that way, since I definitely wasn't the reason Natasha had gone missing. Not on purpose anyway.

Cyrus was about to speak again, when suddenly the sound of something hitting my bedroom window resounded through the room. I jumped in fright, along with Cyrus. We looked at the window in time to see a black object hit the glass, rebound, and go flying back to the ground again.

I glance at Cyrus, but he shrugs in confusion, knowing just as much as I did about the mysterious object. I venture toward the window, nervously peeking out in case it's a Royal Guard. Instead, a see a distraught Landon, standing with a handful of rocks, looking around to make sure my parents couldn't see him.

"Who's there?" Cyrus asks, not too keen about coming closer. I shake my head, turning back to him.

"You should go back downstairs, before my parents suspect you're up here stealing stuff of something. They are suspicious like that," I say. Cyrus looks alarmed, obviously not wanting my parents to think bad about him. Either that or he doesn't want my father to spread the word to his, and get him I'm trouble.

"Only if you promise to come see me later. Tonight maybe?" He offered. I nodded in agreement. Maybe that way I could tell him I'm now mated, and get him off my case. He looks fairly happy about that.

"Tell your parents I'm staying with you or something," I say, as he leaves. He closes the door behind him, but not before giving me a nod and a gently smile.

Once he's gone, I turn back to the window, just as Landon throws another stone. I push it open, and lean out so Landon could see me. When he catches sight of me, he looks relieved.

"Are you okay?" He calls out. He's trying not to yell, or my parents might hear him

"I'm fine. Do you want me to come down so we can talk?" I ask, slightly whispering, but slightly yelling so that he could hear me. He tilts his head, staring up at me in confusion. He's still dressed in the attire he wore to the Alpha Meeting; a tidy, sophisticated suit.

"I'm coming up," he yells back. I roll my eyes, realising he hadn't heard me.

I watch as he pushes his sleeves up his arms, and prepares to climb up the wall. I didn't expect him to get up as quickly as he did, making me move back in a fright, to give room for him to get through the window. I wish he had taken his time, because I enjoy watching his muscles flex.

He clambers into my room awkwardly, his shoes landing on my carpet. He straightens, looking me in the eye.

Seeing him made me feel unbelievably happy. It wasn't just to do with the mate bond, but the fact that I had my friend back, and his father couldn't get to me. He looked good as well, all dressed up and such. Even his hair was combed, which I wasn't used to seeing all that often. Usually his hair is just a ball of fluff on top of his head.

"What did you do?" He questioned, striding toward me. I let him engulf me in a hug, his arms feeling comforting, like home. I breathed in his scent, resting my head against his chest, so I could hear his heartbeat. Just that in itself let all the worries seem to fly away.

"He didn't let me go you know, I escaped," I say, my voice muffled against his crisp, white button up under shirt. He froze, I could tell when his hands stopped rhythmically rubbing my back.

"How?" He asked, sounding apprehensive. I pull my head up, to look in his soft green eyes.

"I had help," I admit. His eye twitches.

"And who decided to help you, my love?"

"Kace. Don't be mad, he just shot two of your Guards so we could escape. Actually, you have all right to be mad," I say meekly, cringing at his expression.

"Althea," he says deeply, his eyes darkening by the second. I know he had warned me about Kace, but I could possibly be dead without him. But something tells me he isn't about to see it from that view.

I backed away, but he continued to advance, looked beyond mad, but at the same time, incredibly sexy. The backs of my knees hit the side of my bed. Staring at Landon, I let myself fall backwards, till I fully lay down, with my feet hanging over the edge.

"Did I not tell you about him?" Landon says, his voice firm, but I was melting in front of him. He leant down, resting his hands on the edge of the bed, not taking his eyes off me.

"Sure you did. He's dangerous, but he saved my life," I find myself saying. Landon sighs, hoisting himself up onto the bed. He calls over my still body, his hands resting on either side of my head.

"You shouldn't be fraternising with anyone dangerous," he says, his breath brushing against my face, his eyes flickering briefly to my lips. I smile at his words, reaching my arms up to wrap around his neck.

He lay his lips gently on mine, and I forgot the strange position we were in. If anyone walked in right now, they would be wondering why the Alpha of this Pack had some random girl pinned to a bed, but I couldn't think of a reason to care.

"I wouldn't call it fraternising," I breathe, as he pulled away, leaving gentle kisses down the side of my jaw. He chuckles, moving his lips to my neck. His change in attitude makes me smile, thinking about the boy I knew before his massive transformation.

I wind my fingers around a few strands of his surprisingly luscious hair. He definitely put something in it today. I shiver, feeling his tongue against my mark. I know he hasn't had experience with other girls before, but it seems as though he's pushing all the right buttons.

I grab his face, guiding his lips back to mine. He kissed me like he had many questions or ask and I guess he does. But for now, I just wanted *him*.

Eventually, Landon pulled away to pull his shirt over his head, dumping it on the end of my bed. It gave me an opportunity to admire his refined muscles. Although really, it is his eyes that are really mesmerising.

He kisses me passionately, moving his lips against mine, but rougher. This fast pace made me lose my breath quicker, as his hands roamed under my shirt, caressing my sides and stomach.

"We should stop. We can't do it here at least," I excuse, catching my stolen breath. Landon nods, his eyes bright. He Rolla over, so he's lying on the bed, and I'm on top of him. I lay my head on his chest again, and he begins to caress my hair softly, and soothingly.

"I love you," I say.

"I love you too," he replies.

Chapter Eighteen

Landon and I decided we wanted to walk together back to the Estate. We had to face Landon's father at one point or another. He definitely wanted me in that prison, and can't be happy that I managed to escape.

It was nice to walk hand and hand with him, reminiscing about the old times.

"Can you believe we used to be just friends?" Landon questioned, gazing out at the horizon. I smiled to myself. I had thought that exact same thing all the time. There wasn't a moment when it wasn't at the back of my mind.

"I know, it's crazy," I reply, chuckling. Our fingers are entwined, as we wade through the grass. Someone should probably tend to this sometime soon.

I glance at Landon, admiring his features. I'm glad he's back. He came back for me, and I couldn't be more grateful. Thinking about this, I wrap my arms around his own arm, and rest my head against his bicep.

"Do you smell that?" He suddenly says out of nowhere. I frown, shaking my head. All I smelt was the fresh grass we were trekking through.

His eyebrows are furrowed, as he concentrates on what he's smelling. He's absolutely disgusted, like he can't believe what he's smelling.

"I don't have your Alpha senses," I say, watching as he starts off in another direction, letting go of my hand. He ignores me, set on finding this strange smell. He looks rather comical, as he treks through the over grown grass, sometimes lifting tufts up to inspect.

"What is it?" I question after a while. He was leading me across the dense paddock, not saying a single word.

"It smells like death," he muttered. My eyes widened. I couldn't smell it, but I knew that he was telling the truth. Generally, an Alpha can smell the death of one of his Pack members for miles. I could tell this was no joke.

I started to hunt around in the grass with him, unsure of what could be uncovered.

"Ah. Baby, you might want to come see this," Landon said softly. I turned around, to see him staring at the ground. He had a look of utter horror on his face. I wandered over to him.

He grabbed my arm as I neared, guiding me to his side. That was how I knew what I was about to see wasn't good. And boy was I right...

A body lay in the grass; I life recently ended. Natasha.

I knew it was her instantly. Her steely eyes were still open, as was her mouth. Her life ended quickly, with a cut to the neck. I could see the blood everywhere. It coated herself, and the grass around her. I had never seen anything so horrific in my life.

I don't know how long I stared at the body, trying to make sense of it all. It wasn't suicide; anyone on their right mind could see that. She had been murdered in cold blood.

"So that solves the mystery of missing Natasha," I hear Landon say. He doesn't seem fazed. At one point, this woman had been his former lover. It would pain me to think about what they had previously done together.

"Who killed her?" I randomly questioned. It was pointless. Landon would be on his way to lock the killer up if he knew. But it felt good to ask. Let him know it wasn't me. She had been killed recently, so the possibility of me being the killer in Landon's eyes is almost impossible.

"I don't even feel any remorse," Landon said blandly. Neither did I actually. Sure, I hated her when I first met her, but I expected to feel sad when I saw her dead body. In actual fact, it didn't even feel very real at all.

Suddenly I hear a noise from behind me. Landon must of also, as he pulls me to his chest, my back against him. Standing in front of us, his Kace.

"I know this looks bad..." he trails off. I blink, unmoving. Yes, standing in front of an Alpha, with a long, sharp knife in his hand, covered on blood. And I'm guessing I know whose blood that belongs to.

"But I did this as a favour, Althea. You pretty much owe me," he continues. He looks as though he regrets his decision. He meekly plays with his short sleeve, sometimes glancing down at Natasha's dead body behind us.

"You killed her?" I ask blandly. I know the answer, I just wanted to have his conformation. Landon remained eerily quiet beside me, like he's contemplating his next move.

"Obviously," Kace responds dryly. He takes a step toward me, but Landon growls threateningly. He sounds so frightening, I feel like maybe Kace would be safer to be around at this point. Not that I have a choice though. Landon's arm is now wrapped tightly around my waist, holding me still like a child.

"Why?" I croak. I feel so much regret right now. Landon was right; I had let a killer out of prison. He had manipulated me into thinking that he is a decent person, who was framed for something he didn't do. He tried to relate to me, in my most vulnerable time... And it worked.

He shrugs. "She was trying to get you framed. She was working with that guy's father." He nods toward Landon. Landon knows what his father is like, and probably didn't doubt Kace for a second.

"So you killed her?" I spluttered in disbelief. He narrowed his eyes, like he had to think about it.

"Well yeah. I found her hiding around your house, like she thought she was some sort of spy," he explained briefly. A spy? She probably just wanted to check on what Landon and I are doing. Well I doubt she will find anything there.

"So you killed her?" I repeated.

"Yeah. She could have hurt you," he stated.

"And why would she matter to you?" Landon cut in... Finally. He let me go, allowing me to pull away from him, and have some distance to think. We were standing too close to Natasha's deceased body, and it was making me nervous.

"Ever heard of vengeance, Alpha?" Kace asked, a slight smile on his face. Landon cracked his knuckles, like he wanted to knock Kace to the ground. I'm all honesty, so did I.

"You're from Kaden's Pack?" He questioned, his voice a low growl. Alpha Kaden is the Alpha of the Vengeance Pack. He's renowned for killing without mercy. Killing at random even. He has haunted my dreams since I was a child. Crossing him would surely be a horrific experience.

Landon probably knew Alpha Kaden by now. Not well of course. Apparently, no one knew him well because he never let anybody. If you got too close to him, he would probably kill you with no questions asked.

But he probably knew what he was like. He must come to every Alpha Meeting, like the others. Except Alpha Grayson of the Freedom Pack. Apparently, he hardly ever shows up...

Having to be in the same room though, as Alpha Kaden must be horrifying. I would have to remind myself to ask him about it sometime later.

"And what would that matter? I practice vengeance because that's what's appropriate in many situations," Kace said casually. He wandered past us, but not too close to Landon. He wouldn't stand a chance against and Alpha like Landon if he got caught.

"Natasha was none of your business. My mate *is* none of your business," Landon snapped angrily. Kace ignored him for a moment. He walked closer to Natasha's body, and knelt beside it. I watch as he pulls a square of plastic material from his pocket.

He then proceeds to unwrap it, till it turns into a large plastic bag like thing. It's like he's done this before, as his fingers work deftly to stretch the lining out.

"What? You want me to admit that I like killing or something? Because that's hardly the case," Kace implied. He lay the bag by the side of Natasha, smoothing out across the Guard.

"It's the only explanation to this, isn't it?" Landon asked in disbelief. How he was able to contain himself from killing Kace at that second was surprising. For once, Landon has decided to be reasonable. Even though, at any second that would probably change.

"Actually, no it's not," Kace said. He wasn't really paying much attention to us. He rolled Natasha's body onto the plastic sheet like thing, so she was face down. He patted the back of her head awkwardly, before standing.

"Go on. Before I-" Landon was cut off.

"Kill me? You don't want to kill me. If you did, you wouldn't find out why I did this," Kace stated, more amused then anything. He had Landon wrapped around his little finger, and knew it.

"As I was saying, before you rudely interrupted me... Althea saved my life. I was on a death sentence, and she let me go free," Kace began to explain. Yeah, well, I wish I had never have done that now...

"I owe her everything. So, I'm getting rid of anyone who should...I don't know, *get in her way*," he continued. I blanched, Landon blanched. We are both surprised at what he is saying.

Does he plan to be my guardian angel or something? The angel that kills? That *isn't* going to happen.

"Who's next?" Landon breathed out. I gape at him in surprise. How is he not wringing this guy's neck? Does Kace dabble in witch craft or something? Has he made Landon subdued to the fact that one of his Pack members is dead?

Kace stood, grabbing the edges of the sheet. He was getting ready to drag Natasha away, so that no one would find out that he's the killer.

But first, he turned and glares straight into Landon's eyes.

"You Landon. You're next."

Chapter Nineteen

Landon's reaction was instantaneous. One minute, he was standing there, completely fine, and the next he was launching himself at Kace, at just a few simple words.

I watched in horror as Landon pushed Kace down with his body weight, sending them both toppling to the ground. Kace sprawled unceremoniously onto the ground, with Landon not too far from him.

Landon jumped up, grabbing for Kace who rolled out of the way. Suddenly Kace was on his feet; being a smaller build then Landon meant he could move out of the way quickly. He took off at a fast pace run across the field, trying to get some distance between him and the Alpha.

Landon staggered to his feet, looking around for Kace. His eyes were completely black now, his fists clenched by his sides. He was angry, and I knew what would happen if he got a hold of Kace.

Landon shifted straight into his Wolf, knowing that he would have immediate strength over Kace. Even if Kace was faster than him.

For a good five minutes, I stood and watched the two Wolves run around the field; one being the chaser, and one being chased.

"Could you please tell your boyfriend to stop chasing me," Kace asked as he ran past me. He hadn't shifted, using his light weight, long legs and head start to keep a fair distance between him and Landon.

"He's not my boyfriend, he's my mate," I mutter under my breath as a response. Obviously, he doesn't hear me, but I'm guessing Landon does; being in his Wolf form and all.

Step by step Landon is gaining on Kace, who seems to be tiring out. An Alpha's stamina is impossible to beat. I need to take action, unless I want Kace's blood on my hands, and Landon's paws if you will... Even if Kace is a sociopathic murderer.

"Landon stop," I shout across the field. Jumping amongst the action would probably be a foolish idea, so I remain where I stand. Calling out Landon's name doesn't seem to be working out at all.

"Landon, I swear to God, I'll-"

I pause. What would make Landon stop chasing Kace, and listen to me? I had to mention something...

"Cyrus would listen to me," I snap. I don't even have to say it very loudly. Landon hears me loud and clear. He skids to a stop, not too far away from me. He was hair strand away from catching Kace; in figurative terms.

In less than a second, he had turned from his Wolf form, and into the man in familiarised myself with. Completely naked and everything. He glowered at me, his eyes slowly melting back to that warm brown colour I knew so well.

Kace, noticing the absence of a blood thirsty beast from behind him, also came to a stop. Although, he made sure he was far enough away from Landon to eliminate *some* danger. At least he was clothed.

Making sure my gaze didn't stray, I remained a steady eye contact with Landon. "You're being unreasonable."

"Unreasonable? He wants to kill me," Landon growled. He shot a glare at Kace, who returned it. He has too much pride.

"Cover your junk man," Kace muttered sourly, referring to the naked Landon. Was he really testing the Alpha's patience now?

"Make me."

"Maybe I will."

"Fine."

"Good."

"I will you two shut up? This isn't the time," I snap, shutting up their bantering. I took a couple of wary steps towards Landon. "We aren't twelve years old you know..."

I grab Landon's hand between my own, getting his attention.

"Let's just get him to the prison. We can talk back at your estate," I tell him promptly. I'll feel a lot safer when we aren't out in the open. Even if Landon's father is possibly back there. It doesn't matter. "Just don't go killing him okay?"

Landon seems to like that idea. But Kace doesn't.

"No. I'm not going back there," he dismisses quickly. He takes an unsure step backward. He then looks at me, like I've betrayed him. "I'm not here to hurt *you* Althea. Don't you get that?"

He sounds hurt, and it makes me cringe.

"You killed someone Kace, we can't just let you go free," I explain in earnest. He shakes his head frantically, as Landon turns to approach him. But he doesn't make any move to run away again.

"Althea..." he breaks off, as Landon takes a hold of him. I can only imagine how hard he is trying not to snap Kace's neck. Honestly, I would feel the same way if he had threatened to kill me, and had already killed one of my Pack members.

Landon holds Kace's hands firmly behind his back, making sure he doesn't run. But it's obvious that isn't Kace's intention. He didn't want to run from me. He wanted to stay near me; that was why he didn't run further then the field. He truly thinks he is indebted to me.

"You can take me in, Althea. But he will come for you," Kace warns lowly. I narrow my eyes at him. "And *he* won't be as merciful as me."

***

I sat on the edge of Landon's bed, my head in my hands. He was looming somewhere across the room, thinking.

Kace was below ground. Not in the morbid way, but worse. He's locked in the prison. What scared me about that, was his lack of resistance. It was like he *did* mind being taken in, he just wasn't about to do something about it. In a way, he's smart. But his words about someone coming for me made me slightly uneasy.

Who could he possibly mean?

Landon stands by the bedroom window, gazing out. He's deep in thought.

"What now?" I ask blandly. He turns his head to look at me, soft brown eyes meeting mine. We are in his bedroom, with the door locked. His father isn't home, but he warned me that he would probably be soon. He wouldn't touch Landon, but I don't trust his motive with me.

If my speculation is correct, he was trying to get me framed for Natasha going missing.

"I honestly don't know," Landon mumbled, walking toward me. As he moved, it allowed me to see over his shoulder, at the clock mounted on the wall. The time usually wouldn't matter to me, but today it does.

"I completely forgot," I yelp, jumping up. I scramble to snatch up my jacket. Landon grabs hold of my arm, stopping me from rushing past him. "What's going on?"

"I told Cyrus I would see him tonight," I explain, brushing a piece of hair out of my face. He's probably waiting. Landon's face screws up at my words. It's obvious he isn't happy about me seeing Cyrus. That's obvious.

"I have a feeling you won't just be *seeing* him," Landon commented sourly. I raise my eyebrow at him. "No Landon, I'm going there to look through his window, just to *see* him..."

He doesn't like my sarcastic reply. I pull away from his grip, and walk to the door.

"I promised I would see him. It will be the last time, because I'm going to tell him I'm mated now," I claimed, swinging the door open. It's true. It's time to finally end it with him, so I can move on with Landon.

"You don't want me to come with you?" Landon asks, handing my shoes before I can run of without them. Balancing on one foot, I slip a sock and sneaker on. He will just make things worse; I can see it now...

"I'll be fine, you stay here, and make sure your father doesn't come and kill me," I say lightly. I was joking, but Landon looks serious. I deftly tie my shoelaces, and stand up. Landon till looks a little uneasy about me leaving.

"It's either this, or continue and get mated to him," I exclaim. Knowing he will hate that even more than an encounter with Cyrus, I feel more confident. I give him a swift kiss on the cheek, and head off down the hallway, hoping no Guards will appear out of nowhere.

***

The walk from Landon's estate, to Cyrus's took a good forty-five minutes. I vaguely remember him giving me his address. He loves a few streets from me, so I'm happy to avoid my own home.

I walk slowly down his street, looking out for number 35A printed on a letter box. It ends up being on the left side, the numbers printed on a tin letter box.

I wander curiously down the paved driveway, ignoring a neighbour of his, watering her garden. She eyes me suspicious, but doesn't say anything. Noticing the sky, it doesn't look as though she really needs to water her petunias; the clouds are heavy with the next shower.

Cyrus's house is exactly what I would have picture. Neat; like him. It was painted stark white, with a tidy deck outside and large windows. I jog up to the front door, hoping his parents aren't home. An encounter with his father would probably lead to some sort of awkward conversation.

89

I knock on the sturdy look, waiting for someone to answer. I had to knock three times, before I heard noise within the house, alerting me that someone was actually in there. Then the door swung open, and I came face to chest with Cyrus.

I blinked, at the half naked torso. Cyrus was only sporting a pair of unbuttoned jeans. He looked surprised to see me, his dark blue eyes widening.

"Althea? What are you doing here?" He asks quizzically. I frown.

"You said we would meet tonight. Remember?" I question. I wanted to slap him over the head, but he did it for me. He smacked his palm against his forehead, like he was just remembering the important detail.

"Shit Al, I'm sorry. I completely forgot," he mumbled.

"Occupied?" I ask. His face drains of all colour, leaving him unnaturally white. He shakes his head, rubbing the back of his neck. I noticed he does that when he's uneasy.

"Can we talk again tomorrow? I'm feeling a little sick, really need some slee-"

"Cyrus baby, come back to bed," I feminine voice said from inside the house. My heart dropped, and I think Cyrus's did too.

I pushed him by his shoulder, so I could see exactly who was standing there. And I couldn't believe who I saw...

Chapter Twenty

"You bitch," I snap. I stormed into Cyrus's house, not even caring about the fact that I'm intruding.

"Althea. What are you doing here?" She asked.

"I thought you were my best friend Missy...What the hell?" I growl. I am seeing red. Actually, I am seeing my former best friend standing in one of Cyrus's shirts, looking at me like she has been caught doing the worst thing a best friend could do... Oh wait.

"Let me explain," she says, taking a step away from me, hoping I wouldn't notice. I wasn't even upset right now; just furious. I'm not even mad at Cyrus. But the sight of Missy makes me want to attack someone.

"Explain what? You're banging the man you *knew* I was supposed to mate," I say lowly. She swallows, glancing over my shoulder, trying to summon Cyrus to help her. Soon enough, I feel his hand on my shoulder, getting my attention.

My hands are clenched by my side in a tight fist, so I hardly register what I'm doing when I swing a punch at Cyrus's face. I *had* indented for him to get a good smack to the nose, but instead he caught my fist in the palm of my hand.

"Althea, you need to calm down," Cyrus said softly, letting my hand drop. Calm down? He expected me to calm down after I walk into this? I'm not at all mad at Cyrus...In fact I couldn't blame him, even if he did lie to me. It was Missy that is truly grinding my gears at this point.

"I didn't think you would mind, considering you're with Landon now," Missy stated. That couldn't possibly be her excuse.

"You should have told me," I mutter, backing away. I practically run out of the house before she could do anything, or say anything to plead her case.

I hardly notice the rain on my back as I jog down Cyrus's driveway. It had to start raining now didn't it. This means I'm running home to Landon, in the pouring rain.

A sudden strike of thunder makes me jump, making me come skidding to a stop. The sky looks menacing, like it's purposely trying to make my day even worse. But nothing could make this worse.

Then I see something at the end of Cyrus's driveway. A black SUV was parked there, window wipers moving quickly across the front windows. The other windows are tinted, so I can't see who is sitting in the back of that thing.

I approach it nervously, knowing that cars like this aren't seen around here very often. Hopefully I can just walk straight past it, with no issues. That would have been a great idea, if I wasn't the kind of person to be an idiot and slip over into the puddle by the cars wheel.

I lift myself out of the puddle, watching the water drip from the front of my nice shirt. Even the ends of my hair are now drenched in the rain water. I wipe off the some of the water from my legs, as I hear the car door open. With this heavy rain, it probably won't make a difference in me trying to dry off.

"Need some help?" A deep male voice asks from above me. I turn my head, looking up toward the sky. The man towers over me, not looking at all phased by the rain battering down on his head. He looks oddly familiar, but I'm pretty positive I don't know him personally. The look in his black eyes suggest he doesn't know *anyone* personally.

"I'm good," I mumble, stumbling to my feet. I didn't take the stranger hand, because I knew better. When I turn around to face him, I notice his intimidating height. But that's not what scared. It's the fact that I *do* know who this man is. Everyone knows who he is.

Alpha Kaden of the Vengeance Pack.

This man is hated by everyone. They call him a demon. If you ever get to see him, and live, you're lucky. This is because his motive is to kill, and that's all. He's what parents tell their children about to scare them before bed.

He's said to be the last person you see before death.

So, you can imagine how terrified I am, to meet his dark, smouldering gaze.

"Althea, I'm glad I caught you," he says breezily. He leans casually against the car, his midnight black hair and dark trench coat taking the brunt of the heavy rain. I'm not glad he caught me.

"What do you want?" I question angrily. His smile widens, like he's sharing an inside joke with himself.

Some myths I heard of him when I was back in school, was that his handsome face is just a mask, and underneath is an ugly devil of a wolf. I didn't believe it though, looking at his face now. He looks to real; and it's frightening.

"I could just be here to say hi, you know," he chuckles. Even as he pushes his hair from his face, it's casual. But I can still tell he's doing it on purpose, since everything he does is purposeful. Maybe he's trying to lull me into a sense of comfort. Not going to happen Alpha.

"Everyone knows your presence comes with a catch," I say knowingly. He nods at that, looking fairly glad.

"You're right."

"So, what is it? I haven't killed anyone, so you're out of luck buddy," I snap, taking a step back. He tilts his head to the side. Surprisingly, he stepped back also, and opened the door to his car. He motions for me to step inside, but I hesitate.

Just looking inside, at the leather interior is tempting. I'm starting to feel the rain seep through my clothes and onto my skin, making it cold and clammy. He was giving me a look, that told me that he had seat warmers.

"We have something to discuss. I would rather not do it in this weather," he said nonchalantly, waving his hand at the inside of his car. I clenched my jaw. I couldn't get in there. It could be some sort of trap, where he plans to kill me.

"I'm going to walk home. Whatever you have to say doesn't interest me," I growl. I spin around to walk away, but his hand lashes out and grabs my forearm, stopping me. I wince, as he turns me around to look at him.

"Get in the car. Because I told you to," he mutters lowly in my ear. I cringe. I had no choice. I was stuck in an Alphas grip, with no chance at escape. And his Alpha also happens to be a murderer in every right. No wonder the Alpha of the Purity Pack despises him so much.

Reluctantly I clamber into the car, with Kaden beside me. He closes the door with a slam, and the car zooms off. I can't see who's in the front seat because it's closed off, but I assume it's someone in Kaden's entourage.

"Why are you doing this?" I question, as soon as we had hit the road. Kaden was staring straight ahead, a grim look on his face.

"I told you we needed to talk," he mumbled. I could hardly hear him over the pounding of rain on the roof of the car. The doors were locked, so if I wanted to jump out of the car at any time, it wouldn't be possible.

"Has this got something to do with Landon? Because if it is, leave me out of this," I growl, folding my arms over my chest. I didn't want to show him that I'm nervous. At any point, he could reach over and end my life.

"No, not particularly."

"Then what is it? What reason do you have to be so elusive?"

"A man in your prison has killed recently. I need you to give him to me?" He said suddenly. My eyes widen, as I know exactly who he is talking about. Kace.

"I can't. He's a probably for the Power Pack, not for you," I explain. At least that's what Landon told me; after he got mad at me for letting him out of prison. Which I now take full blame for.

"Anyone who kills is my issue," he breathed.

"No, I can't...And I won't," I say. It didn't seem as though he needed much convincing. His face went void of all expression, and his shoulders went tense. He thought for a moment, then turned to look at me.

"You won't help me, that's fine. But don't say I didn't warn you," he stated. That made my heart stop.

No, he's getting in your head, Althea. He wants you to help him.

"Just take me home."

And he did. He drove me all the way back to the estate, in complete silence. I could only hope he took this as a loss, and wouldn't continue to harass me about it.

"Goodbye Althea. Should see you soon I believe," was Kaden's parting words, as I hopped out of the car. I hope not. I slam the door, and he drives off quickly. Only his tire marks were left, and I hoped that would be all.

***

Landon was doing work in his office when I went back up the stairs. His dad would be home soon, so I went to warn him that we should probably stay back in his room.

"How did telling Cyrus go?" Landon asked, as I flopped down on the chair beside his desk. He was writing stuff down on paper, and it look fairly important.

"Fine," I mutter. There's no point telling him exactly what happened. He would probably do something irrational to Kaden, and probably start a war between our Packs. That's definitely the last thing I want.

"You took a while, everything okay?" He asks warily. I glance at the clock. I've been gone two hours. Time flies. It didn't even seem like I was gone that long at all. Landon reaches forward and grabs my hand between his own.

"Kace was moved to solitary confinement," Landon said. My eyes widen. "What did he do?"

"He murdered his cell mate in cold blood. The security guards reported him chanting your name," Landon says, his words chilling. I swallow. I suddenly felt unsafe having him living underneath me. Maybe I *should* let Kaden have Kace.

"He doesn't want to kill me, he wants to protect me," I explain to him. He looks disgusted by that. "I don't like the sound of that Althea..."

"Neither do I. Hey Landon? Do you think you could tell me what Alpha Kaden is like?" I ask. He gives me a strange look, like he's uneasy. I can tell immediately that Kaden isn't his favourite person.

"He isn't my favourite wolf within the Alpha meeting," he drawls. I can't help but chuckle a little. He does seem very intimidating, even to an Alpha of the Power Pack. The Power Pack are supposed to be the leaders of all Packs around. It's always been that way.

"I hope you never have to meet him," Landon says, pulling me over to him. I clamber onto his lap, wrapping my arms around his waist.

"Me neither."

Chapter Twenty-One

I have something to show you, today."

I glanced up. I am lying in bed, the sheets over my legs. I am currently reading a book Landon had snuck from his library for me last night, before we went to bed. It's quite old, but a good read.

I had woken up earlier than Landon this morning. Not wanting to wake him, I decided that the book would be a better choice.

Now he stood at the end of the bed, pulling a t-shirt over his head. I couldn't help but enjoy the view though, my gaze peaking over the top of my book. He slowly pulled the end of the shirt down his toned torso, watching me.

"And what might that be?" I question. I close the cover of the book, and lay it by my side. Landon smiles brightly, and I can instantly tell he's excited about something. Problem is, I'm not the biggest fan of surprises.

"I guess you'll have to wait and see," he says slyly, giving me a wink. I roll my eyes and slide out of bed. He was combing his hair back with his fingers, as I strolled over to him.

"Can you at least tell me what it involves?" I ask sweetly, wrapping my arms around his waists. He smiles down at me, and shakes his head, making me sigh. There is nothing worse than wandering into a situation you're unsure about. Lucky for Landon, I trust him with my life.

"All I'm going to tell you, is that it's a special location," he lets out. I frown, my I thought you showed me all your *special* locations back when we were just friends," I muse. He used to tell me everything. I could hardly remember the days when I was only his friend, and crushed on him desperately.

"This one I kept all to myself. I was going to wait until I found my mate, and now I have," he murmured, giving me a kiss on my forehead. I close my eyes, and rest my head on his chest, feeling the rhythmic beating of his heart quite comforting.

***

Avoiding his father, Landon and I snuck out of the palace, after having eaten some breakfast. And as we walk out of the ground, I feel anxious. And this wasn't because I was worried about Landon's father finding us, or his guards reporting us, but because Landon was taking me somewhere special to him.

This officially meant he was ready to full admit that I'm his mate.

"I don't have to close my eyes, do I?" I say, fully expecting him to do something cliché like that. He looks down at me, his arm wrapped securely around my waist.

"Maybe," he says, before looking back at where we were walking. I narrowed my eyes at him, even though he couldn't see that I was doing so.

We walked down a familiar path for a while, the morning sun warm on our faces. It felt nice to walk and not be worrying about anything in particular. I could be worrying about the guards seeing us, and alerting Landon's father; but I wasn't. I could even be worrying about Kaden and Kace, but they weren't on my mind at this point.

I was just happy to be out with Landon.

***

We had walked far from the village I lived in, and now my legs had started to get sore. It had to have been at least an hour since we left the estate. I was dying for a break to sit down or something, but Landon was unrelenting with his long strides.

"How long till we get to this special place?" I question, dragging my feet. We were trekking through grass now. Landon insisted he owned the land, and that was okay. Personally, I would rather be walking on a road at least.

"We will be there soon, I promise," he says, glancing down at me. His hand held mine, guiding me through the long grass that brushed up against my legs.

"Somewhere over there," Landon said suddenly, lifting his free arm to point toward something in the distance. I squinted at the sun, trying to see what he was pointing at. Then I did.

97

A massive, dark forest was clumped densely to the right of my view. I don't usually come to this side of the Pack. I always got told I couldn't go over here, so having this privilege gives me this good kind of feeling.

How did you find this place?" I ask quizzically, as we make our way closer to the dense mass in the distance. Landon smiled secretly, like it was something I was supposed to know. I *am* hi mate now, and he promised to share this with me after all...

"I have my ways Al, don't even worry about it," he stated with a smile. My heart skipped a little when he called me Al. It's been awhile since he's done so, since everything has been a lot more serious than usual. I squeezed his hand a little, deciding not to question what he was saying.

We trekked through the grass for another good twenty minutes, before I could feel the shade of the trees on my face. After a long walk, my feet ached, and I was sweating profusely; so the shade was a welcome relief.

"So, this special *location* of yours is in here?" I quiz, looking apprehensively into the forest. Landon started to walk ahead of me, confidently striding into the forest like it is nothing. I have never really be too keen on the whole forest thing, especially what's in it. I may be a Werewolf, but some things in there make me quite uneasy.

"Indeed, it is. Care to join me?" Landon asks, pausing in his steps when I didn't respond. He turned and gave me a raised eyebrow at me once he saw how I looked at that forest.

"Scared?" Landon asked, when I wouldn't move an inch. He held a hand out to me, trying to entice me in with just a look. I narrowed eyes at him, not wanting to admit for a second that something like an unknown forest was frightening me.

So I take an uneasy step toward him, one tentative foot in front of the other. As I make it to his side, he rests his arm around my neck, and we walk together into the forest.

The deeper in we walked, the darker got the shadows around us got, and the more nervous I began to feel. There was a clear path forged from Landon I had guessed, but it was as though the trees were beginning to close in on us.

"Are we close to this *location*," I asked, after I had stumbled over a log a few seconds earlier. Landon gave me an eager not, and I could finally tell that we were getting close, just by gauging his reaction.

"Want me to close my eyes or something?" I ask jokingly, but when his expression morphs into one of excitement, I suddenly realise my statement has been taken seriously.

He makes me stop by grabbing my arm. Nervously, I close my eyes, feeling his warm hands go over my eyes, just in case I might look or something.

Slowly but surely, he begins to lead me back to the path, telling me every now and again when to step over something, or walk around it.

"Okay, you can open your eyes now," Landon says eventually, making me stop in my tracks. He removes his hands from my face, letting me see exactly what was in front of me. Well, after my eyes had adjusted to the light...

In front of me was something like I had never seen in my entire life. My whole life I've been stuck inside the Power Pack, having never been allowed out to see another Pack until my visit with to the Wisdom Pack. I've never even been able to step inside a forest, since I've always assumed the Freedom Pack was the Pack with all the woodland area.

But here, took my breath away. I small pool of water was situated toward the left of the clearing, with the clearest blue water I have seen. To the right, was patch of fine grass, lined by a few of the bushes native to the forest.

"It's stunning," I hear myself, not even registering what's coming out of my mouth right now. My first instinct was to stand in that patch of grass, and dig my toes in, or lay down. Or maybe even walk to little pool area, and test out the temperature with my fingers.

"Can you see why it's special now?" Landon asks from beside me, having watched my reaction to his special place this entire time. I closed my mouth, that had been hanging open. I was so shocked, and awed by this place to even notice how stupid I probably look right now.

"Thank you...for taking me here," I murmur. Slowly, I stroll over toward the patch of the grass, crushing the pure green strands with the bottom of my shoe.

A waft of air blows up from beside me, as Landon strolls over and takes a seat beside me. He glances up at me, patting right beside him for me to sit. I do so, enjoying the soft grass beneath me.

"You know, I thought about bringing you here a lot while we were just friends," Landon admits. I absorb his words, as I watch him pluck a clump of grass from the ground.

"Really. Why?" I question lightly. Landon closes his eyes for a moment, thinking. I stay silent beside him, my heart speeding up a bit. Did he like me back then as much as I had?

"I've thought you were special for a long time Al. You've never been just my friend," he said, looking up at the sun. His words make my heart flutter again. He doesn't look my way or anything, so I don't suppose he wants an answer to his statement.

So instead, I lean over and lay a kiss on his lips. It's short and sweet, but effective.

"What was that for?" Landon asks, as I rest my head on his chest. I shrug. "Just for being here, with me."

Landon lifts my chin up, and kisses me once again. His lips are so soft, and his tongue so smooth I realise I don't want to stop kissing him. But at that point, and Landon's hands slipped under my shirt, caressing the small of my back, something slipped into mind.

"Kaden came to visit me," I say in between kisses. Landon doesn't stop at my words though. Instead he rolls over so I'm lying upon the grass fully, while he's on top of me.

"Who's Kaden?" He asks blandly, pulling away from the kiss. I run my fingers through his soft hair, as he kisses down my jawline.

"Alpha Kaden," I mutter. And he freezes, his lips hovering just above the base of my neck.

He lifts his head to look me at me, his eyes no longer that soft brown colour I love, but a pitch black.

Chapter Twenty-Two

"I'm sorry, what did you say?" Landon questioned again, like he couldn't believe what he has heard. I smiled meekly, my face turning red under his scrutinising gaze.

"Alpha Kaden. He talked to me about Kace," I admit. Landon visibly tenses up at the sound of the delinquent's name. I assumed he would have pulled away at this point, but instead, he had flipped me over, looming over me.

"And what did Kaden say?" He questioned. I blinked.

I knew that it would be smart to tell Landon about Kace. But the thought of him giving Kace straight to Kaden himself scared me. Even though Kace had killed, basically right in front of me, I couldn't bare to think about what Alpha Kaden would to do him.

I often hear rumours, mainly surfacing from the Purity Pack, about how someone would die from Kaden. Torture is a term used often, and I have a belief that only certain people deserve such treatment. And Kace isn't one of those people.

"It was nothing," I find myself saying, watching Landon's reaction nervously. He narrowed his eyes at me, and I knew instantly that he didn't believe me. Nothing with Alpha Kaden is just *nothing*.

"Althea, don't try me," Landon wanted lowly. His grip on my arm tightens to almost painful, but I don't move, not wanting to admit anything. He wasn't hurting me to the point of absolute pain, he was just ensuring I would submit.

"I'm not, Landon," I mutter, pulling at his harsh grip. His jaw clenches, and I know he's beyond mad. So mad I'm not sure if it's possibly to get him back to the point he was moments ago.

"Tell me what Kaden wants, or I'll go down and snap Kace's neck right now," Landon threatens. His lips are hovering above mine, and I contemplate kissing him just to see if it will calm him down.

101

I sigh in defeat. I was stuck in what to do. Either way, he is probably going to die. So, I do the only thing that came to mind. I kissed him.

At first he was tense. He just let my lips touch his own, without even reacting. Not being insulted, I try coax him with my lips, not being able to move my hands because he still held me down.

Eventually he gave in, but didn't relax, kissing me with a sort of brutality I wasn't used to. But I excepted it, I embraced it. I wasn't used to him having such angst, so this was unexpected, and I had to admit, kind of nice.

"Tell me about what Kaden wants, Althea," Landon says between kisses. I could feel all my doubts flood out of me, as Landon's hands roamed my body. I was beginning to be unable to think straight, and I knew that's what Landon wanted. Suddenly it dawned on me that kissing him probably wasn't the best idea.

"He wants Kace," I murmur, out of breath as Landon rocks is body against my own. His lips were in my neck, my hands were in his hair.

"Did he say anything else, Althea?" He questioned. He had briefly pulled away to talk, but I soon used my hands to push his head back down to my neck. I am needy for his kisses.

He continues his assault on my neck, his hands under my shirt, caressing my stomach and waist. But as Landon kissed me, Kaden suddenly came into my mind again, and I couldn't get him out...

His dark, cruel eyes. His attractive features, he most definitely used in his favour, against innocent girls. His condescending tone of voice. And his words, his threatening, well put together words.

"He said..."

I trailed off. Landon pulled away from me, looking down at me with an insistent gaze.

"He said he would see me again."

***

Landon's Point of View

I walked into the room, slamming the door closed after me. It's dark in here, but I can see him clearly. He it's under a dim light in the corner, rocking back and forth on a chair.

"Landon, it's been awhile," he says, his voice distractingly optimistic. My stomach turned, seeing his endless pool of black eyes stare straight at me. I never liked Kaden.

"You weren't at the last Alpha meeting," I say sourly. Neither was Alpha Grayson, of the Freedom Pack, but he never shows up. Kaden sits forward, hands laced together. Seeing him made me think of Althea. If he had touched her...

"I had other things to do that were of higher importance," he replies. I scowl. I know exactly what that means. He was killing someone probably. It seems like that is all he ever does.

"You talked to my mate," I stated, getting straight to the point. Kaden smiled lightly, knowing this is what I had called him to talk about. I wanted to make it clear to him that talking to Althea is something he will never have the opportunity to do again.

"Indeed, I did. Very attractive girl, isn't she?"

My jaw clenched, and my hands slammed against the table that separated us. Kaden didn't even flinch at the loud sound. I could tell he was enjoying this, but his words angered me beyond belief.

"An attractive girl I want you to stay away from," I said lowly. Kaden laughed, a loud, obnoxious laugh.

"Or what, Landon? You're a new Alpha. Wouldn't want to do anything stupid, by starting a war with the Vengeance Pack, would you?" He teased. I let it a deep breath. As much as admitting it annoyed the hell out of me, he was right.

"All I want, is for you to stay away from my Pack," I say. Kaden stood, matching my height.

"You know I can't do that," he murmurs.

"Please. Althea wants nothing to do with you." I tell him. She doesn't. I will make sure she doesn't have to even think about Kaden ever again.

"Oh really? I'll never be able to see that gorgeous body of hers ever again? I won't be able to touch her again?" He questions. I clench my fists together, refraining from jumping at him, and striking him in the face. Kaden just laughs.

"I wonder if she tastes as good between those legs as she looks," he said. That was it. I leant over the table, grabbing Kaden by the collar of his shirt. No one is allowed to talk like that about Althea. Just hearing his words had me seeing red.

"That's it Landon, get angry... Kill me," Kaden continued to tease. I wanted to. I wanted to end his life right then and there, but deep down I know that what I planned to do isn't what a Power Pack Alpha should do.

"Hurt me, young Landon. Give me a reason for vengeance," Kaden muttered. He was smiling wickedly, daring me to make a move, which he could retaliate from. I let him go, giving in a good shove so he stumbled backward toward the wall.

"You're not having anything from my Pack," I spat. Kaden straightened up, his expression still annoyingly happy. I wanted to knock that smile straight off.

"Including Kace," I add. Kace is my business. He is my business because he came near my mate, which I can't have.

"You're a new Alpha, Landon, so I'm going to give you some important information," Kaden said lowly, his voice basically a growl. I fold my arms over my chest, waiting for him to tell me. Whatever it is, I couldn't care less.

"I am the Alpha of all Alphas. I don't expect you to understand, but I will do whatever I please, so your demands don't affect me in any way. I won't touch your mate... for now. But Kace, is *my* business."

And without, he left the room.

Chapter Twenty-Three

Althea's Point of View

It has been two days since the Kaden incident.

Landon has been acting a bit strange lately. Distant. I knew he had talked to Kaden recently, but he wouldn't tell me what had happened. I even brought up Kace, and what would happen to him, but he just dismissed me.

I have decided I am going to confront him about this. He is in his office right now, working. His father has gone away on a business trip, so we have the place to ourselves.

And I am beginning to feel the loneliness.

So, I wander down, taking the stairs two at a time. But as I get closer, I begin to slow down. What do I say to him? I hardly confronted him about anything when we were just friends. Maybe I had told him what girl he shouldn't bother going after, but that is all.

I peek my head around the corner, seeing Landon stooped over his desk. He just sat there, not moving at all. It is obvious that he isn't doing any work, because he is using both of his arms to prop his head up, that he held in his hands.

"Landon?" I say warily. I don't move from my place in the doorway. He is visibly upset, by the looks of it. He doesn't even turn, or speak to acknowledge me in the slightest.

I amble closer, reaching my hand out to touch his back. I do so, gently. He flinches, a shiver rippling under his skin. Again, he doesn't make any move to look at me.

"Is everything alright?" I ask softly. He makes some sort of noise that confuses me. Does he want me to leave or something? Too bad, I am not leaving until I get some sort of an answer. So I round the desk, pulling up a stray chair for me to sit on.

105

He is covering his face with his hands, so I can't see his expression; which is probably one of annoyance. He is looking down at his desk, that is bare of any paper. I have to know what he is thinking right now.

"I am fine..." His curt voice cuts me off. I had been reaching for him, wanting to make some sort of physical contact. I try not to feel slightly offended by this. I have to remind myself that he is my mate now, and that I have to deal with whatever issue he throws at me.

"No, you're not," I say curtly. I may not know exactly what is wrong, but I know a sad Landon when I see one. So, being brave, I reach out and grab his hand, wrapping my fingers around his own. He doesn't move. I had actually expected him to move away from me for whatever reason. So this is a pleasant surprise.

When he looks up at me, and what I see takes me by surprise.

His tears.

His eyes are bloodshot, and filled with unshed tears. A single tear runs down his cheek. The scene instantly breaks my heart.

Wordlessly, I stand up, and round the desk, so I come to stand beside him. I may not know why he is crying, but what I do know, is that I need to be there for him no matter what the situation is. He pulls me onto his lap, so I am straddling his hips.

"I've failed you," he whispers, leaning his head against my breasts. I close my eyes. His words cause an unknown pain to strike my heart. Why would he say that. I stroke his soft hair to try and soothe him. Even his soft sobbing makes me want to join him in his sorrow.

"No, you haven't," I murmur. Aside from my remorse, I was feeling confused. Landon couldn't do anything to fail me. Unless of course he cheated on me or something, but he would never do that...

"Kace..." he says against my chest. My eyebrows furrow. Kace, I hated to be reminded of him. The man who thought that he owed me his life, when in actual fact, I couldn't care less what happened to him, as long as he didn't harass anyone else again.

"Kaden..." Landon continues to say, in a pained voice. The more he talks, the more confused I become.

"Landon, what are you talking about?" I question. He breathes out onto my chest, making me shiver. I can even feel his wet cheek pressed against me.

"Kace has escaped. And I think I know who is responsible," Landon said. He lifted his head, matting my eyes. I wipe his tears away, and it's like I see a new man there. He looks mad, that's a given...But he also looks determined.

But the fact that Kace has escaped gives me chills. Who knows where he is right now. He could be out there, plotting my death right now. But no, he can't be. He owes everything to me. I shouldn't be worried at all, yet the idea of him coming back for me again scares me more then anything.

"It's okay. Who cares what happened, he's gone now. Out of sight, out of mind," I struggle to say. But even saying that, Kace lingered in the back of my mind. His cheeky smirk would haunt me forever. Even Kaden would haunt me. His power over all the packs was worrying.

"I will always have to deal with Kaden," Landon complains. I roll my eyes. I want to tell him to suck it up, but he still looks visibly bothered. So, I do what I know what will truly calm him down. I kiss him.

His lips are warm, and slightly salty from his tears. I never want to see him cry again, because it breaks my heart. He is pouring all his angst into this kiss, and I let him, even responding to his vigour with my tongue.

"Why do you always have to distract me?" Landon questions through the kiss, squeezing my waist gently. It makes me jump, rubbing my thigh against Landon's crotch. He groans softly in my ear, and I begin to feel a fuzzy feeling begin to consume my stomach. Pleasing Landon is something I had thought about many times before we were mates, but the thought always made me blush and shy away.

"I am taking your mind off of Kaden. Seems as though you are spending more time thinking about him, then you think about me," I joke, running the tips of my fingers through his hair. He smiles, kissing the tip of my nose.

Even though I can feel how turned on he is against my inner thigh, he is being decent, and am glad for that. I will know when I will be ready, and even though I feel it will be soon, I can't cross that line right now until the circumstances are right.

"You know, I have wanted you since we were young," I say quickly. So quickly, I am at first sure Landon hadn't heard what I had said, until his face lit up with a right smile. I felt colour seep into my cheeks, and I tried to hide my face from his view.

"What do you mean, wanted me?" Landon questioned, his smirk bound to scare my mind as much as Kace's has. I shake my head at him, pretending like I didn't know what he was talking about. But in actual fact, I didn't want to tell him the truth again.

"You liked me didn't you. More than a friend," he said, making me hide my face in his neck so he wouldn't see my expression. He laughs warmly, his hands stroking my back.

"Even though I was ugly, and useless?" I hear him ask. I pause.

Did he really just say that? I lift my head up, giving him a glare, thinking he is joking. But he looks completely serious.

"You weren't ugly and useless. In fact, you were more than I could have ever wanted. You still are," I tell him. I hope he saw that his looks meant nothing to me. Now, and back then. His change didn't change my views in the slightest.

"In fact, I thought you were very handsome," I state confidently. I grab his face, and he laughs, like he doesn't believe me at all.

"You have always been beautiful. I bet you wouldn't be mine if your father let you date that boy way back,' Landon said, completely straight faced. I blinked. Levi? the boy I liked back when I was thirteen? I hadn't actually liked him, I just made it seem like I did so Landon wouldn't think I was desperate.

"You're kidding. You're bringing up Levi?" I mutter, rolling my eyes as he screws his face up.

Levi had been a friend of my mother friend. He was attractive, and every girl liked him. But he had more dick in his personality, then he did in his pants...

"I was unbelievably jealous," Landon admitted. "I thought you and him would be mates one day, and I would be forever alone."

I lightly punched his shoulder. He had to be kidding, I mean I thought he didn't think about think about that kind of thing at all. Ever.

"Well I am yours now. Forget Levi, and anyone else," I tell Landon, resting my forehead against his.

Chapter Twenty-Four

I tread softly to the door, trying to make my footsteps as quiet as possible. I am trying to get out of the room without waking Landon up.

I make it to the door, and turn around. Through the haze of darkness, I can see Landon laying on his back, arm slung over his eyes. He seems to do that a lot when he sleeps. I don't want to leave him, but I think I slept most of the night with my mouth open, because my throat is completely raw, and I need a drink of water.

I leave the room, and silently close the door behind me.

I pad down the steps on my tiptoes. I don't need to worry about waking anyone else up, but the sound of my footsteps seems to echo.

I make it down to the kitchen, and the turn the light on. It blinds me for a second, because I have been immersed in darkness for some time. I blink away the feeling, and wander toward the fridge. I find a bottle of chilled water inside, and crack the lid open.

It feels nice to finally get water to soothe my throat.

As I sip my water, I stare out the window. I don't see too much, just the pouring rain hit the window wildly. Storms make me uneasy, I have to admit. I turn my back to the window, and rest my elbows against the bench.

I had just put my bottle down, and was about to turn the kitchen light off so I could go back to bed, when I heard a large sound resonate throughout the room. I turn around wildly, but there was nothing there.

"Thunder," I mutter to myself, running a hand down my face. I watch the window, waiting for a strike of lightening, so I could count the seconds between the thunder.

Then suddenly, a face appears at the window, shadowed by the night.

I scream, ducking down behind the bench. My heart beats quickly in my chest, as I kneel awkwardly on the floor. What was that? I take a moment to regain my breath, before scolding myself for being such a baby.

What if it is a guard who got locked out or something? And I am here hiding for my life.

I peek out from behind the bench, to see there is no one at the window. Had I simply imagined it? Kace is getting to my head.

But then, the face appeared again. This time I didn't move. I remained where I stood, completely overcome by fright.

He stares at me with eyes as black as night. His forehead is creased, which allows me to immediately tell that he is pained. I notice that he is shivering on the other side of the window, as he is completely drenched in rain. As horrifying as he is to look at, I can't take my eyes away from him.

Warily he brings his hands up, so they are in my view. They are covered in blood, dripping from his fingertips, and down his wrists. Looking into his eyes, it's like he almost can't be believe that he did it...Whatever *it* is.

I am suddenly faced with a tough decision. Let in the crazed wolf who might have killed someone outside. Run back upstairs and tell Landon. Or go back to bed and convince myself that I am for the first time, experiencing a lucid dream.

I like the latter.

I turn on my heels, going to leave the room as fast as possible, when a hard knock on the window made me turn around again. I know I shouldn't, but the knock was so loud, the sound gyrated in my ears.

Kace was writing something on the window with his fingertips with the blood on his fingers. I blinked, trying to make out the wobbly lines of smeared blood across the glass. I was reading it backwards, but as soon as Kace finished tracing the last S, I knew exactly what he meant.

Cyrus.

My cheating, almost mate.

My eyes widen, as I register the severity of the situation. Kace beckons me over with urgency. All I can think, is that he has done something with Cyrus, and I have to find out what.

I stumble forward toward the window, each step getting me closer and closer to the window, till the glass was all that separated us. Looking at him made me want to thrust my fist straight through the window, and into his face.

He opened his mouth, shouting something at me. I couldn't hear what he was saying through the glass, and over the thunder. I knew I had to open the window.

Using whatever semblance of strength that I could muster, I unlocked the window, and pushed it upward.

The sound of rain is louder now, pattering against the concrete outside. But what scares me the most, is the fact that Kace now has full access to the house, and me. Instead, he takes a step back, putting some distance between us.

"It's Cyrus," he says, in a cool, calm voice. I swallow. As much as I should be concentrating on pushing the fear away, all I was noticing was the trail of blood on the concrete, leading off into the darkness.

"What did you do?" I question, my voice breathy. Kace holds his hand out; the hand covered in blood. I pull back.

"You need to follow me, Cyrus is in trouble," he insists. And I believe him...

How could I not, when the possible killer is standing right in front of me.

So, without thinking, I follow my will and clamber out the window, knowing I would alert the Guards if I took the door. Kace tries to help me out, but I brush him off; I don't want anything to do with him right now.

In my night dress, I follow Kace into the rain and darkness. The cold rain hits my arm, but I push through. I stumble across the sloppy ground, splashing through puddles as I try follow the incriminating path of blood.

"Where is he?" I yell through the rain, the gust of wind forcing the rain toward me. Cyrus is ahead, and I use him as a guide. The light from the estate is getting further and further away, as we reach the end of the property.

Kace glances behind us, his eyes widening.

"We need to hurry, this way," he says. Ignoring my protest, he grabs my hand, and drags me toward the exit. I know where he is taking me...Toward the edge of the cliff that Landon's family built their empire upon.

"Althea!" I hear a familiar voice cut through the night. It's Landon, I know, but I can't turn around to look, due to the force at which Kace is dragging me.

The edge of the cliff comes into view through the haze of rain, lightening on the horizon lighting up the area every so often.

And what I see beneath a tree, is a body, sprawled on the ground.

I rip away from Kace to run toward it. It is definitely Cyrus; I can tell instantly.

"Cyrus!" I shriek, landing on my knees beside him. He is unconscious, blood seeping through his shirt. I tear at it, trying to pull the cotton apart. My fingers, numb from the cold fumble, but eventually I expose his chest. I can see in the poor lighting, the hideous gauge in his chest, still spilling out blood.

"I had to do it..." I hear Kace say from behind me. I swallow the bile raising in my throat. I knew it was him...But he isn't important right now, Cyrus is.

I grab Cyrus's face between my hands, his cold, lifeless face. There is no colour in his cheeks, and his eyes are shut. I can't feel anything right now, but I know tears are streaming from my eyes.

I stand, turning as I do to say, "Why did you do this?"

"I told you, I would do anything for you," he insisted, taking a step toward me. His back faces the light from the estate, so I can't see his face at all. It is like I am staring into a dark abyss.

"What makes you think I would want him dead?" I question loudly. I can start to fell fury peak through my misery, and if I don't calm down now, I am afraid I will act on it.

"He cheated on you!" he yells at me, like I am stupid. Like I should know that cheating warrants death.

I grit my teeth, fighting to see him in the poor light.

"Vengeance huh," I mutter.

I lunge at him, hands bared to wrap around his neck and kill him. It is all I feel at this point. I want him dead. I want him to join everyone who he has killed in the past.

He catches my hands just in time, trying to divert my attack from his face. But kick my foot out, striking his knee. He groans, letting my hands go. I take this chance to push him toward the edge of the cliff. Not enough to send him tumbling over the edge, but enough to scare him.

He stumbles back, and suddenly I can see his eyes. A look of betrayal...Like he can't believe I am doing this to him, after he committed his life to be my aid. But he doesn't stop his retreat, his foot slipping on the wet grass.

And that was the last I saw of him.

He completely fell backward, his back hitting the edge of the cliff, before gravity threw him completely off.

I screamed, as loud as I could. I didn't even have time to register what was happening before I felt hands on me. Warm, large, familiar hands of my mate.

I turn around and fall into his chest, stunned. I know he is looking over my shoulder, seeing where Kace had fallen moments ago. He must have seen...He got here just in time.

The cliff leads to a deadly fall onto sharp rocks below. There is no chance Kace could survive.

"Come on, we need to get you inside before he comes," Landon said quickly. He grabbed my legs, swinging me up so he was cradling me. I look up at him, seeing the rain coming off his face.

"Who?" I ask, my voice shaking.

"Kaden."

Chapter Twenty-Five

Landon came back into the room, holding a towel.

"We can't just leave Cyrus out there," I insist. I sit on a chair in the kitchen, soaking wet. Landon had taken me inside despite my vicious protests. Cyrus is outside, needing urgent medical attention.

"He's dead Al," Landon grumbles. He kneels down in front of me, wiping my hair back with the towel. I don't care that I'm a mess...Sometimes when your emotions are too high, you don't even register the tears running down your face.

I push the towel away, which makes Landon growl. "You'll get sick if you kept this up."

"We can't just leave him out there though! What if he's actually alive, and we are letting him suffer?" I question, exasperated. Landon sighs, trying to wipe my bare legs of the dirt and water that recently covered them.

Once he had cleared all the dirt off my legs, he said, "My guards will get him in the morning."

"In the morning?" I question widely, completely shocked that he wouldn't see this from my perspective. I know Landon never liked him, but this is *way* too far, even for a protective Alpha.

His eyes darken.

"Althea, I don't think you understand-"

But I cut him off. "No, *you* don't understand."

Landon narrows his eyes. He throws the towel over my shoulders, but I shrug it off. He isn't listening, and it's getting on my nerves.

"You're in a lot of trouble Althea," he murmurs, standing up fully. Seeing him stand in front of me fully like that is nerve racking. Not because I think he will hurt me, but because he is so much taller than me, and asserts so much dominance.

"Stop saying that?" I demand. He furrows his brows in confusion.

"Stop saying my name like that. You're making it sound like..." I break off. I sound stupid.

He sighs, holding his hand out to me. I take it warily, letting him bring me to a stand. He engulfs me in a hug, despite the fact that my clothes are soaking wet. He doesn't care, so I embrace him gladly.

"I'm just worried about you Al," he mutters lowly, kissing my hair. I sigh out deeply. We are both stressed. I no deep down that Cyrus is dead, but I feel numb. It's like my mind hasn't accepted it yet, but my body has. I feel weak, drained almost. I just want to curl up into a ball and forget about the world and its entirety.

"What's going to happen now?" I ask warily. I don't want to know the answer because I already know. But maybe if I hear it come out of Landon's mouth, I might actually be able to believe it.

He sighs, running a hand down his face.

"Kaden," he mutters. I know that. Whatever tie Kace has to him, it's bound to be enough for him to get mad at me. And a mad, murderous Alpha isn't something I want to think about right now.

"Maybe he won't know for a while. It will give us time to get out of here," I say quickly, as if time really is about to be a major issue for us.

Landon looks conflicted. He doesn't look like he feels bad in the slightest. I don't blame him; I blame myself for not caring as well. I know later I will sit down and think about the real burden of Cyrus's death, but right now adrenaline pumps through my veins.

"And go where? I can't just abandon my Pack like that," he tells me. That's a good point. His father is retired now, and not just *anyone* can take over his role.

"Then I need to go," I say, my voice breathy. My heart drop at the thought of even considering it. Landon's face is instant disgust-not wanting me to run away either-but I am faced with little other choice. Landon grabs my hand in a firm grip.

"That's not an option," he tells me, his eyebrows furrowing together. He holds my face up, so I am forced to look in his eyes, and face the scared look that hides beneath them. "We are in this together remember, so there is no negotiation when I say that you are not going anywhere."

I smile. And for the first time in a while, I feel complete.

Landon, still holding my face pulled me closer, so that our lips met.

His lips pressed against mine are searing hot. A sudden moment of realization dawns on me. I am ready for Landon, and by the feel of it, he is too.

He picks me up and takes me upstairs. I am not aware of anything around me, until I am being lay on the soft surface out Landon and I's bed. He lays between my spread legs. I concentrate on his comforting green eyes I know so well.

"Don't be scared," he whispered in my ear. And I am not. How could I be when my first time is about to be with my best friend/mate?

He leaves soft kisses down my neck that make me shiver. Experimentally, I attempt to pull his shirt off, but he has to finish the job for me. I run the tips of my fingers down his muscular back.

He undresses me piece by piece, making sure I am comfortable with everything item that he rids from my body. The awe on his face is obvious, as he takes in my blushing figure. He may be my mate, but seeing him look at me still makes me nervous.

Taking some control, I roll Landon over so I am straddling his waist. I slid down his warm body, introducing myself to the rest of him that I haven't explored. His chest, his stomach. I fumble with the button and zip on his pants, so he helps me again.

Kaden is now out of my mind completely. And I am glad. This is a welcome distraction from reality.

Landon pulls me back up before I can explore further. He turns us around, so once again I am below him. We are both naked, and I try to come to terms about what is about to happen.

This could have been Cyrus and me if Landon had never mated me. I shiver at the thought.

"You can back out of this if you want," Landon says, nervously noticing my expression. I shake my head at him. There is no turning back now.

"Shut up and take me *now* Landon, and don't regret it," I whisper in his ear. He smiles, and thrusts in cautiously. Checking if I am okay, he thrusts again, more confidently.

At first, I feel pain, but his soft whispers in my ear, and the feeling of his fingers against my skin soothe me, and begin to feel myself enjoy it. I enjoy the feeling of him inside me for the first time ever. *Now* I feel complete.

And the feeling doesn't stop. It doesn't stop until it hits its peak. Landon hits his climax at the same time, as I call out his name, and moan in his ear. The feeling is like nothing I can ever explain, but it's more pleasure then I could ever imagine experiencing.

Landon rolls off of me, breathing heavily as he does so. I regain my breath, before rolling on my side to look at Landon. His face is covered in a slight sheen of sweat. He turns and smiles at me.

"I love you," I tell him confidently. And I mean it.
"I love you more."

Chapter Twenty-Six

I woke up confused, feeling sore across my whole body. The I remember what happened last night. I smiled. I turn over, ready to greet Landon, except he's not there.

The absence in the bed sent a shiver down my spine. Where could he be?

I say up, looking around. My clothes lay discarded on the floor, but I decided I wanted to put clean ones anyway. I felt exposed, as I got out of bed and hunted around the room for cleaner clothes. I may have been naked before Landon yesterday, but today is a new day, and I'm still shy

Having still not shown himself, I decide it's time to head downstairs to try find Landon. He's got to be somewhere around here. Maybe he had Pack business he needed to deal with.

I stalk down stairs, listening out for any trance of him. Once I'm downstairs, I hear soft voices talking. Is Landon by the front door? Maybe he was collecting Cyrus's dead body. I shiver at the thought. I really want to see Cyrus before he is given to his family.

I turn the corner, to see Landon and another man at the door. Landon leans against the wall, his head in his hands. The other man stands tall, his arms held behind his back.

The man that stands I don't recognise. He's larger in build then Landon, which immediately makes me aware that he is an Alpha. His eyes a hard blue. He looks tough, and it's unnerving.

He looks at me as I walk over, and goes to move toward me, but Landon's hand reaches it and stops him. I don't move, unsure of what to do. Landon looks over at me, his eyes lined red. I frowned at him.

"Althea, this is Kael," Landon says hoarsely. Kael? It dawns on me who is standing through there. Alpha Kael...Another feared Alpha within the community.

He nods at me. "Of the Discipline Pack."

I know. I should have guessed as soon as I lay my eyes on him. He runs a Pack of order and control. Everyone in his Pack is trained to be the best fighters, while at the same time following military like orders. And Kael is the leader of them.

Although my Pack is known for brutal strength and ability to fight, we don't understand discipline like his Pack members do. He is the police of this world.

"Why are you here?" I find myself saying. I don't know why, but it came out rudely. He is here for a reason. Why else would he be here? He should be within his own Pack, ensuring everything is going how it should be. Instead, he's here.

Landon looked grave. That's how I knew he has gotten bad news.

"We heard about what has happened...With the boy," he said solemnly. I blinked. He knew? He had to mean Kace, who had toppled downhill by his own means.

I glanced at Kael. "Kace, you mean?"

He frowned. Landon shook his head at me, his eyes widening. What? What did miss....

"Kace who? I meant Cyrus, the boy found dead on this Alphas property," Kael said. I glanced at Landon, who was looking down at his feet. He was getting blamed for the death.

"He didn't kill him...Kace did!" I insist. Kael still looks confused. Does he not understand what I'm saying? I'm telling him who murdered Cyrus, and he is looking like I just admitted I've seen aliens in my life time.

"Who is Kace?" He questions.

"He's from the Vengeance Pack...He killed Cyrus, not Landon," I insist. Kael doesn't look convinced, and my heart begins to sink. Why isn't he listening?

Landon still doesn't look up, knowing the weight of the situation. Kael says, "Well, Alpha Kaden said he witnessed the killing. We need to take him into questioning before we can extend our investigation."

I stare at the Alpha in disbelief. What about Landon's Pack? What would the do if they found out their Alpha is being taken to trial for the murder of one of their fellow Pack mates. There would be anarchy.

Landon still doesn't say a thing. He is willing to take the fall for it, if it means I won't get prosecuted, I can tell. He knows my hands were all over Cyrus, after Kace had killed him.

"I did it," I find myself saying. Landon looks up in disbelief, while Kael screws his face up in confusion.

"If you search the body, you will see my DNA is *all* over him. I killed him, not Landon," I say quickly. I don't even register the words that are coming out of my mouth by this point. All I know is that I will not let Landon go to jail, and maybe even be given a death sentence for something he didn't do.

That I didn't even do...

"Althea stop," Landon warns.

"I'll sign a full confession. On paper," I tell Kael. That's how the police work right? That's what he wants from me?

"You're admitting to murder?" He questions in disbelief. I can tell by the look in his eyes, that he has never come across someone like me in his whole reign as Alpha.

I nod, but Landon quickly steps in. "You will not arrest her."

"If she is admitting to it, I *have* to take her in for questioning. I have no choice," Alpha Kael says, exasperated. Landon steps in between Kael and I, trying to ensure he can't get to me.

"What about me? What if I confess too?" Landon questions.

"Well, well, well, what do we have here?" A voice suddenly says from behind Kael. We all turn in surprise, to see a smug looking Kaden outside.

Landon growls. "You have no right to be here."

Kaden looks at me. His eyes are so cruel. I wonder briefly if he has someone. Is he mated? Does someone love him as much as I love Landon? I can't imagine.

"In fact, I've brought evidence to this case," he said. Evidence? He wasn't anywhere near here when this all went down. He has no right to come in here with whatever lies he's about to spread. But unfortunately, he's the Alpha of Death, and whenever there has been a murder, he's jumping on the opportunity in a second.

Kael looks confused. He's the only one who matches height to Kaden, and the intimidation factor. "You said you witnessed the murder?"

I growled lowly in my throat. He witnessed nothing. He is a liar, and as much as I want everyone here to know that, I have nothing to back my case. Kaden, on the other hand, holds up a small dagger, blood drenching the blade.

"Is that..." Alpha Kael trails off. *He must have gotten it from Kace.*

"And where I found this, will surprise you even more," Kaden said. My heart dropped, as his eyes met mine, and his lips curled into a cruel smile.

"Althea, want to tell us why your mother found this in your bedroom?" Kaden asked. My mother? My blood ran cold. My mother didn't even know if I was alive. Did she seriously think I was a murderer?

I glanced at Landon, to see him frown. "How could she have that knife, if you saw me kill him?"

"Maybe I saw wrong. I'm just saying, if Althea had this knife in her room...." Kaden trailed off, but we knew what he is thinking. He's framed me. Because that's what the Alpha of the Vengeance Pack does. He lies, and he frames to get what he wants.

Wordlessly, I allow Kael to snap the cuffs over my wrists. It's better than Landon taking the fall. And anyway, I'm sure I'll get out of this once Kael sees that I'm not guilty.

As I'm being walked out of the house, Landon is yelling abuse at Kael and Kaden together. He's pleading with them to let me go, to take him instead, but the damage has been done.

I'm about to slide into Alpha Kael's car, when Kaden grabs my shoulder to stop me, leaning in to whisper in my ear.

"I'm going to bring you down for what you did to Kace..."

Chapter Twenty-Seven

"This in unnecessary," I mutter. Kael stands on the other side of the bars, giving me a sad look. Maybe he knows deep down I didn't do it. Still, he had the audacity to lock me up in a prison cell for the night.

"I have to. We have someone to come speak to you tomorrow," he says.

Speak to me? I have nothing to say. I have admitted to murder, and now, I just need to prove that it wasn't actually me, but Kace.

"Who?" I question. Kael shakes his head at me, and I realise that I'm not going to find out today. Not knowing is going to eat away at the curious self within me. Is it a forensic investigator or something? Someone to test Cyrus's body to see what had really killed him.

"Sleep Althea. We will speak in the morning," Kael said, walking toward the door. I let him go without responding. I'm not mad at him of all people.

I'm mad a Kaden.

How could he do this to me? I hadn't intentionally tried to hurt anyone...I didn't even ask for Kace to become my slave or whatever he thought he was. I just want to live happily with Landon, and not have to worry about anything else.

I lie down on my bed for the night. The pillow is as rock hard as the pathetic mattress beneath me.

This bed wouldn't be so bad if I had Landon here. I feel tears at the back of my eyes, but I held them back. I will only feel worse if I sob because of my problems. I choke back the pain, and try force myself into a sleep.

And eventually I did, Landon the last thing lingering in my mind before I passed out.

***

I wake up to the feeling of someone watching me.

I sit up, rubbing my eyes as I look to see why I feel such a thing. And I see a man sitting on a chair he pulled up right outside of my cell. He watches me curiously.

"Rylan," I break off. "I mean, Alpha..."

The Alpha of the Purity Pack stands in front of me, watching me with curious blue eyes. He's a lot different up close to what I've seen on the television. He seems to radiate. I want to lean out of my cell and touch him to see if he is as perfect as he looks. Is he even real?

"You may call me Rylan. No need for formality at this point," he said. Even his voice is soft, causing a shiver to run up my spine.

"Why? Because I'm a criminal?" I question. He laughs lightly, shaking his head at me. He scoots his chair closer to the bars of my cell. I remain sitting on my bed, which is on the opposite side of the cell.

"I know a criminal when I see one, and you're definitely not it," he says gently. Despite his calm persona, his unrelenting eye contact makes me nervous. It's like he's searching through my entire soul with just his pretty irises.

I sigh in relief. "Then why aren't you letting me out then?"

He sighs too, but he sounds strained.

"Kaden has created a web of evidence against you. Unfortunately, my word isn't enough to be presented in court," he tells me. My eyes widen immediately.

"But you're an Alpha. Shouldn't your word overrule any jury?" I question. His solemn look answers my question. My heart sinks, carrying the weight of the situation. I may be in prison for the rest of my life at this rate.

"No, unfortunately. But I will do anything to get you out of here," he says honestly. Despite the situation, I feel a little bit of confidence come back. The Alpha of the Purity Pack as my lawyer has got to be something to be proud of.

I glance down at my hands. "So, what do you suggest we do then?"

"I know the Judge that you will be dealing with later. I can talk to him," he says. Is that it? Will that even guarantee me a chance out of this Pack?

He notices my expression. "I won't stop until justice is served."

I thank him, shaking his hand through the bars.

And then he's gone, and I'm left wondering if he was ever actually here. Or if I was dreaming.

***

Later that day, I was transported to the court house to await my trial. Here, things need to be done quickly. Maybe they think I'm going to kill someone else in that time.

I'm tempted, that's for sure.

Two guards parade by my side, their guns holstered, but still there. Where Alpha Rylan is, I'm not sure. His emotional, and possibly physical support would mean a lot right now.

What I've gathered, being transported through the Discipline Pack, is that everything here is so uniform.

As I pass by people, they don't even look at me. They look straight ahead like I don't even exist. They walk in straight lines, and their talking is kept very minimal. I want to reach out and touch one of them to see if they will react. But every time I step out of line, I'm prodded in the back to be reminded of my place.

I can't begin to imagine what life would be like to live here.

Suddenly, out of nowhere, a thick rock flies towards me. I duck, as natural instinct. It goes straight over my head, hitting the guard behind me.

I look to see where it had come from. A girl stands on the roof of one of the many buildings here.

She's beautiful, standing over everyone as if they cease to exist. Her long blonde curls wave in the air, while she begins to climb down the building, using the fire escape as leverage.

"Jada!" Someone screeches from our left. The girl, landing on two feet, turns to see who had called her name. Jada, it suits her.

She looked at me, giving me a wicked smile that can only mean trouble. The guard beside me, checking to see if the other guard is okay, notices her, while other guards run at her from the left.

"Follow me," she says. For some unknown reason, I follow her. I don't even consider the fact that I'm bound to get in major trouble from Alpha Kael. Possibly, I could be stuck in this Pack having rehab or something.

We run to the right, her in front of me. I watch her feet as I run, trying to hop over obstacles with the same skill she is. It's more than obvious that she's escaped authority before.

"Stop," I rasp after a while. "I think we lost them."

She skids to a stop, turning to me. Her eyes are a furious green, her cheeks stained pink from the run. She laughs, which makes me laugh as well.

"Jada," she introduces, holding her hand out. I take it and shake. "Althea."

"I know. I've heard a lot about you, and I'm honestly intrigued," she says. She leans against the wall, holding her hand against her chest, breathing heavily, but not nearly as heavily as me.

I frown. "Intrigued?"

"Just by looking at you, I can tell you didn't murder that boy," she says, raising her eyebrow.

I glance down at my body. What's that supposed to mean? I like to think that I have an intimidating factor about me. That is a lie...

"I think I may have killed one of Alpha Kaden's Pack members," I told her. I don't really know what Kace's relationship is to Kaden, but it must be close if Kaden is going to such high lengths to ruin my life.

Jada's reaction surprises me. She jumps up from where she had leant against the wall, the biggest smile on her face.

"You killed the bastard?" She giggles. I try smother my smile, but it's impossible. "Who, Kace?"

"Yeah Kace? Glad he's gone to be honest, you've done this world a favour."

Her words make me think. Did I really do the world a favour? I mean, Kace was a criminal. I decide I don't want to mention the fact that I let him out of prison, or the fact that he actually indebted his life to me before he fell down the cliff.

"So why did you save me?" I question her. She smiles wickedly again, and I can tell immediately that this girl usually gets up to no good.

"Let's just say I'm 'with' the Alpha. And I'm going to convince him that you really aren't that bad," she said devilishly. She is with Kael? The callous Alpha that dragged me here yesterday? These two don't really seem like they would be a match made in heaven.

"How are you going to do that?" I ask. She shrugs, waking around in a little circle coyly.

"I have my ways. I think he likes me," she mutters.

My eyes widen at her words. There is no way I'm going to question her on what she means about that.

Suddenly she seems to notice something, her eyes glued to my neck. I stand stock still when she approaches me, flicking my hair back across my shoulder.

"You're marked?" She breathes. My hand flies to my neck, protectively covering my neck from her eyes. I nod at her.

She stumbles backward. "How can that be?"

"He's my mat-"

"No!" Her hands fly upward.

Wordless I'm being approached by her again. She grabs my shoulders and shakes me a little.

"How can you be mated? You haven't even met your real mate yet..."

Chapter Twenty-Eight

I furrow my brows, confused. My real mate? Landon *is* my real mate.

Jada holds her hand out to me.

"He will be here, as Kaden is," she murmurs. I don't take her hand. What is this girl going on about? I am mated to Landon, and that is it. There is nothing she can do about it, no matter what she says.

"I'm sorry, I have no idea what you're talking about," I tell her. She narrows her eyes at me, looking me up and down as if I'm some foreign creature she has never seen before in her life.

"Don't you know about mates?" She questions.

"Of course, I do, I am mated after all," I say blandly. She shakes her head at me, running her fingers through her hair as if she can't begin to comprehend why exactly I'm saying these things.

She takes a deep breath. "After the war happened, and Packs formed, the Power Pack were one of the many Packs to believe in military over religion. I had no idea they didn't teach you about mates."

"We grow up, and chose who we see ourselves fit with," I tell her. She slaps her hand on her forehead.

"I can tell you're having a hard time understanding..." She mutters, exasperated.

"How would you know who I'm compatible with anyway?" I question angrily. This girl has known me for a matter of minutes, and now she's telling me who I'm *destined* to be with. Not that it matters anyway, it's Landon's mark upon my neck.

Jada didn't say anything, but instead, grabbed my hand. She dragged back the way we came, dodging the same obstacles with ease. I tried to question her on where she was taking me, but she remained to herself.

"Your mate, I have been friends with for many years talks about you often. You two are mates, I know it," she said, swiftly pulling me around a sharp corner. My eyebrows furrowed. It seems everyone around here knows more about my life than I do.

"Althea!"

I turn at the sound of a male voice. It's Alpha Rylan, storming across the courtyard toward me. He looks worried, like he's been searching for me for a while. It can't have been that long...

Surprised at the sight of an Alpha, Jada lets go of my hands and runs off in the opposite direction, not turning back. So, I'm left alone to deal with the frustrated looking Alpha, who isn't even my own Alpha.

"Where have you been?" He questions me. He's breathing heavily, I notice, when he makes it close to me. I expected him to grab me, so I couldn't run, but he doesn't. Maybe he knows I'm not that stupid. I wouldn't run now anyway, as I trust Rylan more than anyone else.

"Some girl told me I have a mate," I said. The way I said that felt foreign. He nods his head, and for a moment I thought he was going to say Landon's name.

Instead, he says, "Yes, Coen."

I frown. "Who?"

"Coen. A personal Guard of Alpha Kaden," he tells me solemnly. Coen. I have never heard that name in my life, let alone known he would be someone I'm destined to be with.

"How do you know?" I ask. My head is throbbing. If it's the heat, or the information I've been presented with, I don't know. Rylan sighed, like I should know these things about him.

"I'm the Alpha of the Purity Pack. The Moon Goddess tells me," he says. I fight to keep my face expressionless. The Moon Goddess is something that I don't truly believe in, but everyone is different.

He holds out hand out to me to take. I do. "I think we should get this trial over with."

I sigh. He's right. Jada said she would try help, but I don't know how much one girl can do to save me from imprisonment for my entire life.

***

The court house is like nothing I have ever seen before. We have court houses back at home, in my Pack, but nothing compared to this. The interior is frightening. Pictures of past judges hang from the wall. Alphas are usually the judges, with little exceptions. Today, Alpha Kael will be taking my case.

And deciding my verdict.

A jury sits around the edges of the room. They all look uniform, staring at me with disgust in their eyes. I shrink back in the box I've been forced to sit in. I'm even elevated over everyone else, like my sins are being paraded to all that dare look.

Kael isn't there when we arrive. I'm left standing there for what feels like hours, wishing I wasn't. My heart aches for Landon. His comfort would go a long way at this point.

Kaden stands by the door, looking up at me. All I can do is glare at him, even though a lot more would please me greatly. A man stands beside him, dressed in a long coat. He's similar to Kaden, although smaller, with lighter hair. Every Vengeance Pack member looks similar, because there isn't much diversity.

He meets my eyes, and I feel something stir in my stomach. Do I know him?

Suddenly Jada barges into the room. Her cheeks are flushed, her clothes rumpled. She brushes past Kaden without a fear, and stands at the edge of the jury seats. She seems distracted by something.

We meet gazes, and she winks. This makes me relax a little. Did she manage to convince him to let me free? How she could do it is something I don't really want to think about...

Alpha Kael walks in a little while later, fixing his shirt a bit. They definitely were up to something.

I glance at Jada again to see her nodding toward the man standing beside Kaden. He smiles at me, and I know instantly what she means.

That man is supposedly my mate.

Coen.

"Althea," I hear a familiar voice say. I glance down from my box, to see Landon within the crowd below me. He looks at me with a pained expression, but tried to give me a smile.

I smile back, trying to show him I'm not scared. Having to be shouldn't be a thing, if Jada did what she promised.

The court is bustling. Werewolf court rooms require three individual powers to control someone's fate. The judge, which is usually the Alpha. The jury, made up of important Pack members, and the viewers. The viewers get little say, but enough to tip over fate.

But over all, it will be Kael that decides who walks out of here a free man.

The ceremony begins with Kael introducing himself, then me. He gives a brief history of my background, and what I may have done. Supposedly.

He presents the evidence himself, and the suspects. Everyone goes stiff when Kaden's name is mentioned.

This whole thing lasts more than two hours. It drags on and on, Kael mentioning a bunch of Werewolf jargon I'm unsure of.

I keep finding my gaze fluttering back to Coen as Kael talks. He's staring at me blatantly, not worrying about being polite or anything. I'm hardly taking in what Dallas is saying, but at times, it's as if he's batting for my team.

By the time it comes for me to make my one and only plea in my defence, I'm stuck for words.

Everyone turns and looks at me, as I stutter over my words. What should I say.

"I can't be the killer..." Is all that comes out of my mouth. Kael looks at me, his head tilted to the side.

"And why is that?"

"Because Alpha Kaden is more of a killer than me. It's obvious he planted the knife in my house. If you ask my parents, I haven't been home in a long time. I've been spending time with my mate, Alpha Landon. Also, I would like to say that some man from the Vengeance Pack killed Cyrus. You can check Landon's criminal records from the prison below his estate. Kace, is his name. He is dead now. But he killed Cyrus, you will find. I would also like you to know that I have *never* killed before, or even done anything remotely illegal. I am an innocent person, who does *not* deserve to be locked away in prison," I finish.

The silence stretches beyond the court. Instantly, I can tell my word has gotten through to them.

"Right, well, I guess we will take a moment to come to a decision," Kael said. He stood up swiftly, gathering has papers before leaving the room. Discussion began, and I was let out of the tiny box I've been stuck in.

As I went outside to get some air, I hoped I would bump into Landon. I needed to see him to tell him I love him, before Alpha Kael made his final decision.

Instead, I saw Jada.

She ran at me, a smile on her face.

"I think you're going to get out of this alive," she said happily, grabbing my shoulders and giving them a little shake. I forced a smile onto my face, but I'm not so sure.

Suddenly I see Kaden from the side of my view. He strides over, a look of anger on his handsome face. I *hate* to think of him as attractive. I'm sure he belongs to someone else out there.

"I'll give you two a moment?" Jada said nervously, seeing Kaden approaching. I want to tell her to stay, but she skips off quickly. I stand my ground, waiting for him to why to me, and hopefully not kill me.

"Althea."

"Kaden."

"I hope you know that you will pay for what happened to Kace. Whether Kael is the dictator of that, or me," he mutters to me. He's talking lowly so no one can hear his threats, which worry me to the core.

"Back off," I growl, pushing him by his chest. He doesn't even flinch.

"Do you really want to try me?" He questions, his voice dark.

"Kaden, leave her alone."

Kaden turns, and I look from behind him. His personal guard, Coen, approaches.

My mate. Apparently.

Chapter Twenty-Nine

I stand there, staring at the man in front of me. He's tall, well-built and attractive. He has that soft, gentle look about him that Landon doesn't have. But compared to Landon...Well, he can't even compare.

"Ah, Coen. I see you have finally met your mate," Kaden says smoothly. Does everyone know about this, except me? I'm mated, to Landon...Why can't everyone understand that?

Kaden steps back, grabbing the man's shoulder. He pushes him forward, so he stumbles closer to me. I take an apprehensive step back, not wanting to be as close to this stranger. Even he eyes me carefully.

"I'm sorry," he mutters, once Kaden walks away. He is apologising for Kaden nearly killing me, but not for the knowledge they are spoon feeding me.

"What's going on?" I question. He frowns, slight lines forming on his forehead.

"What do you-"

"Why is everyone telling me you're my mate?" I question. He blanches at my tone.

I glance around. No one seems to notice our conversation, despite my outburst. I want to cry, I want to scream. I even want to punch and kick him until he tells me what's going on. But I don't. I remain calm and composed.

"Because you are my mate..."

"No. I have another man's mark upon my neck," I tell him. He shakes his head in disbelief. Without my consent, he brushes my hair back, revealing the mark. The look on his face says it all.

He gently runs his hand over it, making me jump. There is a spark there. An unexplainable jolt between us. I push him away, scared.

"Did he mark you against your will...I'll kill him," he mutters, his face going red in anger. His fists clench at his sides.

"I chose him," I tell him desperately. "Because that's what you do..."

He shakes his head, grabbing it with both his hands. He looks like he's in tremendous amount of pain, grabbing his hair and pulling it as if he's trying to expel bad thoughts.

"You don't just *choose* your mate," he says in between pants.

"What-"

"Can't you feel this?" He grabs my hand, that strange feeling pulsing up my body. I rip away from him, taking a few steps back which he only matches forward.

"Stop-"

"Mates are given to you by the Moon Goddess," he says, his voice so desperate, I feel as though he might cry.

My head is spinning so fast I feel as though I'm about to faint. His words don't make sense to me.

"Coen-"

"Don't you want me?"

"I can't!" I yell at him. I yell so loud that everyone stops to look at us. It even shuts Coen up, as he stares at me with a betrayed look in his eyes. When I glare back at people, they turn back around, pretending they never heard anything in the first place.

"I don't know you," I exclaim. A sudden feeling of calmness settles over me. Maybe I'll be able to face this again without yelling.

Coen's shoulders deflate. "That's because we just met."

"I've already met the man I love. A man I've loved for many years," I say gently. My tone is soft, and understanding. Yet Coen still fights through it.

"How can you love someone, when your mate exists?" He questions, as if my words are completely infallible. The look of loss and misunderstanding is stretched firmly into his features. Despite my confusion, I still feel bad for him.

I brush it off. "I've grown up with a completely different background to you. Choosing your mate has been something I've grown up believing is the only option..."

My words break off, falling away at the edges.

I grab Coen's hands. "And I think I may be pregnant."

His eyes widen in disbelief.

"It's early, but we didn't use protection..."

Coen stumbles backward, the look in his eyes so cruel and torn. He looks me up and down, with a look that is almost like disgust.

"I can't believe you would betray me like this," he says. I shake my head, my shoulders deflating.

"I didn't know-"

"Is everything okay?"

A familiar voice makes me relax. The soft melodic tone of the one man that I am mated to.

Landon.

I spin around, seeing him stride over. He glances at Coen, but seems to brush him off. He instantly wraps his arms around me, drawing me to his chest. Letting him embrace me for a few moments, I slither out of his grip; I don't want to make Coen feel any worse.

"Who's this?" Landon asks, motioning at Coen. If looks could kill, Landon would be ten feet underground. A look of murderous distain on Coen's features makes me shiver.

"Coen," he says, thrusting his hand out. I watch nervously as they shake hands, Landon's knuckles turning white as Coen squeezes them rightly.

Landon draws his hand away, looking impressively calm. "Are you trying to challenge me?"

"No Alpha. I just wanted to congratulate you on your mating with Althea," Coen says smoothly. Landon glances at me, but I avoid his gaze.

"Thank-"

"Good luck with your baby," he finishes, before turning his back on us to walk off.

I can feel Landon's hot gaze on me, but I try my best to ignore it. I grab his hand instead, wrapping my fingers around his own.

"We should get back inside," I say. My attempt to walk away is stopped short by Landon's grip pulling me back. I'm forced to look up at him, his grip under my chin keeping my gaze from straying.

"You know I love you right?"

I smile. "I do. And I love you too."

"And whatever happens in that court room doesn't define you. I *know* you didn't do anything wrong," Landon tells me. His words spread a warmth across my skin, giving me a sudden boost of confidence.

***

I'm back in the box. Kael is here. My fate hangs loosely in the air.

My eyes scan the room for Landon, but instead I find the cold eyes of Coen. He stares at me with something that can only be explained as hatred.

The fact that he is a Vengeance Pack member makes everything worst. If anyone can hold grudges, they can. They turn their vendettas into something cruel and sadistic, and use it in their favour.

He stands beside Alpha Kaden. I hope those two aren't too close, otherwise I'm truly dead...

Dallas clears his throat, ceasing all hum of discussion in the room. I stand up tall, meeting his eyes.

"I have used my time to revaluate the evidence," he says smoothly. Lies. He was out back kissing Jada like Landon said.

"The new evidence that has risen has given me a clearer view of what happened that night," Kael continues. I glance at Kaden to see him frown. Then I avert my gaze to Jada, who winks at me.

What could this mean?

"As the dictator of this court room, I have made my decision."

My heart stops, and for a moment I think I might faint. Everyone in the room leans forward in their seats as they hungrily listen for my verdict.

"With no objections, I announce Althea to be not guilty."

Epilogue

Six months later.

I stand at the window, staring out toward the backyard. Landon and I recently moved here, after his father came back. It's been six months since I was announced not guilty at court.

Things have been simple; Landon, myself and our baby living in a smaller home in the middle of the densest forest in the Power Pack. It's safer here, where Landon can continue his Alpha duties without the risk of his father intruding on our relation.

My hand reaches up, brushing the mark upon my neck. I shiver as I touch it, thinking of Coen. Rejecting him is something I *had* to do. I was right when I assumed I was pregnant with Landon's child. It just wouldn't be fair on Coen to raise another man's child.

And anyone, I'm in love with Landon.

"Admiring the view?" I feel a warm pair of arms wrap around my waist, large hands caressing my large stomach.

"Thinking," I say, leaning my head back onto Landon's chest. He kisses my cheek, also looking out at the backyard.

I twist in his grip, so I face. He's dressed like he's going some sort of raid. He's got his dark clothes on, which suggest some sort of Alpha duty.

"Going somewhere?" I ask. He nods, ruffling my hair.

"I am. Someone spotted Alpha Kaden's car drive into our territory. Thought I better go check it out," he murmurs.

"I had really hoped you'd come back with me to estate to collect the rest of our stuff...Before your father comes back," I say with a sigh.

Landon gives me a sympathetic look. "Sorry to pass on that. You and baby can do it."

We both look down at my stomach. I nod slowly. "Okay."

Landon means down and gives me a swift kiss. It sucks that he has to go out, but I'm glad he's trying to keep Kaden out. I *hate* that guy, and I can't begin to think of anyone who actually can stand his presence.

I grab my coat, and decide to walk to the estate. It's nice stroll through the woods, and I need the fresh air anyway.

Despite the extra weight I carry, I make it to the estate in good time. The place has been abandoned for three weeks now. I've only got a few small things I need to grab before I can leave.

I was just hunting around for a shirt of mine left here, when a knock at the door makes me jump. Someone's at the door, when this place is supposed to abandoned...I don't think anyone should be visiting now.

Nervously, I wander toward the door. Instinctively, I hold my stomach, like I'm protecting my baby.

When I open the door, I'm faced with a girl around my age. She's small; petite almost. Her hair is a light blonde, which hangs around her heart shaped face like nothing I've ever seen before. Her eyes shine a bright blue.

But what really gets my attention, is the fact that she looks absolutely filthy. Her stunning skin is covered with a smear of dirt that travels from her cheek to her neck. Her legs are covered in light green grass stain. Even her hair has a little bit of branch in it.

"Who are you?" I question apprehensively, noticing how she's staring at my stomach. She looks up, her eyes widening.

"You're Althea," she says bluntly. I nod slowly. Does she know me? Because I have never seen her in my life.

"You didn't answer my question," I snap. I didn't mean to sound so bitter. Suddenly her eyes glaze over, and she looks almost regretful.

"I don't know who I am."

Made in the USA
Middletown, DE
20 September 2020